THOMAS CHRISTOPHER GREENE is the author of four previous novels: *Mirror Lake, I'll Never Be Long Gone, Envious Moon* and *The Headmaster's Wife*. His fiction has been translated into 13 languages. In 2008, Tom founded Vermont College of Fine Arts, a top graduate fine arts college, making him the youngest college president in the country at the time. He lives and works in Vermont.

ALSO BY THOMAS CHRISTOPHER GREENE

The Headmaster's Wife

Envious Moon

I'll Never Be Long Gone

Mirror Lake

A LOVE STORY

T. C. GREENE

First published in the United States in 2016 by Thomas Dunne Books, an imprint of St. Martin's Press.

Published in hardback in Great Britain in 2016 by Corvus, an imprint of Atlantic Books Ltd.

1 0 9 8 7 6 5 4 3

A CIP catalogue record for this book is available from the British Library.

Hardback ISBN: 978 1 78239 935 3
Export trade paperback ISBN: 978 1 78239 934 6
E-book ISBN: 978 1 78239 936 0

Printed and bound by CPI Group (UK) Ltd, Croydon, CR0 4YY.

Corvus
An imprint of Atlantic Books Ltd
Ormond House
26–27 Boswell Street
London
WC1N 3JZ

www.corvus-books.co.uk

For my siblings:

Stephen, Kathryn, Maura, Richard, David, and Daniel

Hey, buddy, just write something everyone wants to read, will ya?

—CAPTAIN KEVIN O'CONNOR, QUINCY, MASSACHUSETTS, FIRE DEPARTMENT

Two roads diverge in a wood, and we took the one more traveled by.

—HENRY GOLD, *APPROPRIATING FROST*

If I Forget You

Henry, 2012

On the kind of beautiful spring day where no one expects anything of significance to happen, Henry Gold, a poet who teaches at NYU, finishes class and decides to do something he has not done in years, walk a good length of the city to his apartment. Normally he hops the A train on Fourth Street and arrives within a few blocks of his house. Today he is feeling inspired, as if he has not seen the sun shining in a while, though that can't be true, can it? Hasn't it been a magnificent spring?

At forty-two years of age, Henry Gold is not a famous poet by any stretch, though he won a few awards in his youth and this translated into a teaching career. He has been in *The New Yorker* twice, though not for about ten years. What he is, is a fine teacher. He has an ear for other's work that he doesn't have for his own. He is able to discern a musicality that certain students possess and is able to nudge them in the right direction, for he believes that is all a teacher of writing is really ever able to do.

Henry walks through Union Square Park and then up Fifth Avenue. All around him is the madness of the city, and he sees it today with fresh eyes, like someone who is just visiting here must. Everywhere he looks, he sees something that makes him smile. Even the insanity of midtown, people moving like schools of fish, then stopping all at once and standing in one giant breathing group, doesn't annoy him as it usually might.

Through a V of lesser buildings, Henry spies the Chrysler to the east, his favorite New York landmark. The sun has been arrested in its spire, a kaleidoscope of spun gold.

The day is warm, and as Henry walks, he removes his suit jacket and hangs it over one arm. Passing a playground, he sees a woman dressed in black scolding a small curly-haired child, and Henry cannot help but remember his own mother, his fiery and emotional mother, whose coal black eyes burned hot when she was angry. He remembers his West End of Providence neighborhood, where he was the only Jewish kid. His mother once racing outside in her thick black dress and pinning an Italian bully to the ground, her knees on his biceps, her hands strafing his face and asking him how he liked it. He remembers all his constant embarrassment and how he ran from all of it. Nights when as a child he lay in bed and wished he wasn't a Jew and asked himself why they just couldn't be normal and be Catholics like the other families. Henry recalls his mother saying to him, "Henry Gold, don't ever let anyone tell you can't do something." Her words haunt him, for it is the great failing of his life. Many years ago, someone told him how to do things, and he didn't fight like he should have.

Henry shakes his head. He doesn't want to think about this.

He moves through the crowds on Fifth before the park, the shoppers with their oversize bags in each hand, people spilling out of stores with ornate window treatments, the heart of commerce in the heart of the most important city of the time.

Soon the city opens up once again. Here now is the park, Olmsted's great monument to smart planning: an emerald island in the middle of the concrete one. It is bustling, too, of course, the hustlers and the horses and the pedis all lined up to take advantage of a sunny day. Tourists having their photo taken with the guy dressed as the Statute of Liberty. Henry stops for a moment and studies a chestnut tree in full bloom, golden cones like offerings waiting to be plucked.

Henry has a vague idea about maybe getting a drink. He is feeling bright and wants to be around people. He drifts across Central Park South toward Columbus Circle. There is a wine bar on the third floor of the Time Warner Center that he has been to a few times. It is a good place for someone alone. It is the kind of place where he could sit for hours with a book and a glass of wine.

Yes, this is what he will do. When Henry reaches the plaza in front of the center, for no reason in particular he suddenly stops and turns so his back is to the building. It is just before five o'clock and there is a rush of people. Henry puts his arms up in the air, and it is like standing in the ocean, the waves coming over and then falling back and then coming over him again. This is not a city where people just stand still.

He looks toward the park across the circle and he sees the pigeon. There are thousands of pigeons, but this one is flying right at him with what looks like purpose. Henry smiles. The pigeon is like a missile. The gray bird flies past him, and Henry instinctively turns, and as he watches, the pigeon flies directly into the glass above the revolving doors without braking at all. It slides off the glass and lands on the ground, to the right of the door. People stream out, unaware of the death in their midst.

Just when Henry thinks he is the only one who has seen this, a woman coming out the door stops. She leans down next to the pigeon, which is on its back. She places her hand on its breast. She is well dressed, a gray suit, hair cut in a bob. As if she senses Henry's eyes on her, she suddenly looks toward him, and the face Henry sees travels to him from a lifetime ago.

"Margot," Henry whispers. It is a name he has always loved to say. A name that is sui generis to him, it could only belong to her. He has never known another Margot. It is a name he likes to turn over in his mouth. A tiny poem of a name, how it rises to the *g* and then falls soft as silk to the silence of the *t*.

He sees a flash of recognition in her look, and now he definitely says her name out loud, though it is instantly drowned out in the roar of the city.

For a time that feels like forever, their eyes meet. There is no question now. It is Margot. And in her face, Henry sees that she recognizes him, too. Henry starts to walk toward her, and as soon as he does, she gets to her feet and moves into the roiling rush-hour crowd.

"Margot," he shouts, but she doesn't stop.

She climbs into the yellow cab that is first in the line of yellow cabs. Henry is running now. He is at the window. She looks up at him—those eyes, unchanged, the pale blue of sea glass—and he stretches his hand toward the closed window and the cab lurches out into traffic, merging quickly, a damn sea of yellow cabs, and he tries to keep his eyes on the one that carries her, until he is no longer sure which one it is and a phalanx of them moves up Broadway and out of sight.

Margot, 2012

A tiresome monthly lunch with her mother summons Margot into the city. She is so reluctant to go, she has this fantasy of missing the train. Though she knows what is expected of her. Outside her house, she stops for a moment and stands in her expansive yard, the large Tudor house behind her, and she just takes in the smell of the lilacs. Her husband, Chad, has a mild allergy to them but tolerates a few weeks of sneezing because the smell of them, slightly fetid and soapy but also sweet, she loves more than anything.

Then on the train, Margot is restless and anxious about lunch with her mother. But something else is bothering her, too, and it's hard to put her finger on it: more of a vague unease she has had lately. Perhaps it's only because this is the first year both her kids have been away at school. Alex is in his third year at Wesleyan University and Emma has just started at Miss Porter's. School is out in a week. But then the busy summer will start, a few days home and then Emma off to camp in Maine, the same one she attended as a child, and Alex to the city with friends for an internship. Maybe it's that, how fast everything always moves, life like this train, uncontrollable to her and nothing she can do to stop it.

Or perhaps it's Chad? Sure, he works all the time, and sometimes she wonders if he is the kind of man who has affairs. He always knows her schedule, so she never has an opportunity to surprise him in the city. Perhaps he has a whole life here she doesn't know about. For isn't that the way with men who work in the city and live in the burbs?

Coming through the Bronx now, the train passes abandoned warehouse after abandoned warehouse, broken windows and graffiti. Funny how much trains stare at the darkest parts of America. Places she would never see otherwise.

From Grand Central, she takes a cab to Columbus Circle. Lunch is at Masa. Her parents bought a place on Central Park West ten years ago, top floor of a prewar building overlooking the park. They are seasonal New Yorkers—here for the fall and spring—with winters in Tucson, Arizona, and summers on the Vineyard. Many of the friends in their orbit following a similar schedule, like school for wealthy retired people. Lately, her mother has discovered sushi. When Margot was growing up, her mother practically sneezed at anything ethnic—of course there was no Masa then, with its $450 prix fixe.

Her mother waits for her in the foyer to the restaurant. They kiss on both cheeks. Her mother is immaculately put together, as always, as if an important social event might materialize at any moment. Margot reminds herself to exude energy, and right away she has the sense of her mother appraising her, assessing her, and that after, a full report will be given to her sister, Katherine, as Margot always gets one on Katherine post her mother's lunches.

Do other adult children meet their parents in an atmosphere like a job interview? Like they are trying out for the role, perhaps? Would you be my daughter? Of course, that's absurd, and over a bottle of Corsican white, and the tiniest pieces of the freshest fish imaginable, they talk.

Her mother takes her time but eventually warms to the topic that interests her. It is not a new conversation. They—her parents—are concerned about Chad. He is forty-five years old now, well in his prime, and still mid-level at Goldman. Worse, he is on the sales side, which is less attractive than becoming a partner. Margot wants to tell her mother that Chad is essentially a good-time guy: that the wealthy clients like him because he is funny and amiable and that he loves to drink. Chad has never met a party he couldn't make his own. He is quick with a top-notch cigar and a rabidly funny dirty joke in his back pocket. Besides that, Chad doesn't really like to work. He doesn't have that burn of ambition you need to have to climb to great heights, the burn her father clearly had when he became CEO of the largest soft-drink company in the world in his early forties.

Her mother looks at her across the table between small bites of something incredibly exotic—Margot didn't quite hear what it was. Peekytoe crab, maybe. Her mother's eyes are steely blue, like hers, though colder.

Her mother says, "Perhaps there is something you can do?"

"What do you mean?" says Margot.

"A wife can often be the greatest asset," her mother says cheerfully. "You could do more, you know. Charities. Get yourself out there. What do you do in that house all day?"

Margot considers this. Lately she has been painting again. With the kids gone—except for summer—she suddenly has this sea of time. In truth, she has been busy. There are the normal volunteer things she does, serving on the library board and on the board of a foundation a friend started after her son died of a rare disease. She does Pilates three or four days a week, depending. There is the weekly doubles match with the same group of women. She belongs to a book club, of course, which is more an excuse to drink wine than it is to really engage with literature.

But of all those things, the painting is what gives her pleasure. Margot wanted to major in art in college—but the kids who majored in art, to put a fine point on it, were not like her. She studied art history instead, which at least had the veneer of practicality. Not that a career was something she would ever need to worry about. But if she couldn't paint, she could at least pretend that someday she might be the curator at a museum or run a downtown gallery. Art was the only subject she ever really liked, but she harbored her love of painting like a secret. And the only one to ever see anything she has done is Chad, who will look over the swirling brushstrokes, the abstracts she is into now, and always make some joke about how everything she does looks like a vagina and why is that.

"A secret weapon," her mother says.

"What?" Margot asks, aware suddenly that she had been lost in thought and looking down the length of the dining room to the panel of windows, the ones that look south toward midtown.

"You could be his secret weapon, dear," her mother says. "Never underestimate how important the wife can be."

Margot thinks about this. Perhaps she could do more, especially in the city. Cricket and others are always after her to join this or that board, help organize this gala. And the children always gave her a polite reason to demur.

Margot makes it through the rest of lunch. Her mother suggests they do some poking around in some of the stores in the mall, but Margot is prepared for this. She has made plans to meet a friend for coffee on the Upper East Side. At the door to the restaurant, they kiss again, on both cheeks, and Margot moves through the expanse of mall, down three sets of escalators, and to the front door.

She is just about to move through the revolving doors when something draws her eyes upward. She sees the pigeon then, sees it before it hits the glass. Then she sees it hit and slide to the ground.

Through the doors she goes, and behind her is the rush of air as the carousel continues, people being pushed out into the spring day.

When she was a child, at her parent's giant brick house in Westchester, birds used to fall off the roof, out of the gutters, babies, and Margot would nurse them back to health. Sometimes they didn't make it. Other times she fed them white bread soaked with milk out of an eyedropper, and like a miracle, they grew. In her yard, she would teach them to fly and they would leave her.

Margot kneels next to the pigeon. She is oblivious to the people moving around her. The bird, squat and city-fat, is on its back. Margot puts her fingers on its breast. She feels it heave up, one last time, soft and hard, a final breath. And then the pigeon goes still under her fingertips.

Margot looks up, and twenty yards away or so is Henry. It is an older, stouter version of Henry, but unmistakably him. She would have recognized him from behind, just from seeing him walk. Funny how that works, isn't it? How the smallest of clues can create an entire portrait of someone we know well?

Henry has his suit jacket slung over one arm. He is saying her name. This is a moment she has long imagined, and part of her knew it would happen like this, when she wasn't thinking about it all.

Henry starts to walk toward her. Margot stands, her heart in her throat, and she does the only thing she knows how to do. She moves quickly to one of the waiting cabs. She does not look back. She climbs into it and says to the elderly driver, "Fifth and Eighty-second." He doesn't say anything in return, just starts to inch out into traffic.

And then Henry is in her window. His face. Those dark eyes, his curly hair cut short now, with a hint of silver above the ears. His hand is reaching out to her; the spread of his fingers and the glass separates them. The car pulls away and into the spinning circle, yellow cabs after yellow cabs, and Margot does not look back.

Henry, 2012

Henry stands at the edge of the curb, watching the traffic flow around the circle and then disperse. In the movie version of his life, he would be more decisive. This moment, the one that just passed, would have been handled differently. He would have climbed into the next available cab and pointed to the one that carried Margot and loudly shouted, "Follow that cab." He would have handed over a crisp fifty-dollar bill to the driver as encouragement.

How do you find someone that doesn't want to be found?

Henry has never stopped looking for her. Twenty-one years, and some have slid past faster than others, and in between there has been lots of living, the standard victories and defeats that constitute a life, but Margot, the idea of her, the essential memory of her, has been his one constant truth, like a poem he has committed to memory and holds always in the back of his mind.

He waits each quarter for the alumni magazine to come, and as soon as it appears in his mailbox, he has it open before he even reaches the elevator. Henry scans the class notes to see if she has written in, if anyone has seen her lately. Some small note even that says "Caught up with Margot Fuller recently in New York." He even takes to writing in himself, in case she decides to get in touch with him.

He joins Facebook. He friends everyone he can find from college. He friends friends of hers from those days. Once he wrote a message to a close girlfriend of hers, a woman who still goes by the nickname "Cricket," and no one knows her given name. He said he was trying to get in touch with Margot and any help would be appreciated. In the manner of the technology, Henry could see that she had read his message, but she never responded.

Henry wonders if perhaps Margot has been under his nose all these years. For all he knows, they share a neighborhood—no, that is unlikely. New York can be a surprisingly small town, a web of villages. He sees the same people over and over again. Surely he would have seen her before now?

Standing on the curb, looking out toward the park, Henry is aware of his heart, the steady percussive thump of it. He replays seeing her over and over in his mind. Did he imagine it, or was there something in her eyes when they connected, first when she knelt next to the dying bird and then later when he was less than a foot away from her as the cab pulled away? Was it a longing he saw? Could you even see that in someone's eyes, or is he transferring what he himself felt onto her?

Henry begins to walk. It feels like a long time ago that he left his classroom with this idea he would amble home. It is almost as if his day has been split in two—before Margot and after Margot. Then again, he could say the same of his life, this afternoon's having become simply a microcosm of his entire existence.

On Amsterdam, he stops at his regular Indian place and orders the same thing he always does, the chicken tikka masala to go. At his apartment, Henry eats in front of the television with a bottle of wine, an early-season Yankees game on. He barely watches it. Instead, he has a pervasive sense of loneliness bigger than any he has felt in a long time. He considers his apartment. Two rooms really. A square box. He looks toward the window, where the spring sun has set and the sliver of visible sky is fading to purple.

Tomorrow, Henry decides in that moment, he will go to Vermont and open the camp for the season. He doesn't have class again until after the weekend. Why hadn't he thought of this before?

This idea lifts his spirits a little, the desire to do something, to feel like he is moving forward instead of giving in to the stoppage of his internal clock a few hours ago at Columbus Circle.

Vermont was his father's place. His taciturn, silent Polish father, who cleaned floors in office buildings and factories his whole life, discovered Vermont. Once a summer, the three of them, for Henry is an only child, packed up their car, borrowed a pop camper from someone his father knew, and drove north, where they camped at the edge of a small lake. Henry's mother, who had been born in Warsaw, grew up in Queens, and lived her life in Providence, hated the woods.

But Henry discovered later it was a gift they were giving him, this week, that it was less about the woods and more about showing him that there was a world outside the neighborhood and that he could have it. That he didn't have to stay in Providence. There were possibilities for him. It was why they named him Henry, too. Henry Gold sounded like Henry Ford to his mother. As if he, this child of immigrants, could someday embody the American dream.

Henry has never forgotten the first time he saw dirt roads cutting through the forest. He has never forgotten his father teaching him to fish, riding a canoe out onto the broad expanse of water and dropping a line and reeling it in, a perfect sport for his father, since it was about repetition and silence, the two things he knew better than others.

It was when his father died, the summer Henry turned thirty-four, that he decided to buy his own piece of Vermont. He spent a year looking before he settled on a six-hundred-square-foot seasonal cabin at the end of a cow path through the woods and built into the side of a cliff, the lake coming right up to the deck that extended off the front of the house. The place was small and ill-built, but it looked out clear across the small lake toward a rising hillside of pines, birches, and maples, and the water itself was clean, clear, and cold.

Yes, Henry thinks, tomorrow, Vermont. This decided, he pours himself some more wine. On the television, the Yankees are losing badly to the Orioles. He watches for a moment and tries to summon his old love of the game. But it eludes him now, and the euphoria of thinking about opening the camp fades quickly, and the loneliness returns, sweeping over him like a cold wind.

Henry stares at his phone. He desperately doesn't want to be alone all of a sudden. Sometimes he wishes he was like some of his male colleagues in the department, who don't think twice about using their station as a platform for seducing young women. It is such a cliché and farce, he thinks, but yet, like all clichés, true: Women will sleep with you just because you are published, as if somehow your minor (to them, major) success can be conferred upon them by their giving themselves up to you.

If Henry had been like that, he could simply send a text right now, and perhaps one of them would come over. He could read to her and then they could make love. It would be lovely to share a bed with someone again. Just to feel that warm body next to his when he rolled over at night, the timeless refutation of the darkness of it all.

But Henry knows only one way to love a woman, and that is completely. Sure, some of his students have come on to him, some of them blatantly; others he has been oblivious to until someone else pointed it out. He has always kept a certain remove, though, and maybe that's because of how he was brought up, the strength of his own mother tempering, always, how he relates to women.

Once, when he was around twelve, a group from the neighborhood went to Narragansett Beach, about forty minutes from Providence. He doesn't remember how they got there, and it wasn't a school trip, since it was the summer.

What Henry does remember is the ocean on that sun-soaked day, how it twinkled as far his eye could see, the crashing of the surf, and the gang of neighborhood boys, mostly Italians who had accepted him into their circle solely because he was good at stickball, jostling and roughhousing at the edge of the endless sea, each of them mildly afraid of the ocean's power.

In front of the boys were the neighborhood girls—in particular, Lani Moretti, Henry's first crush. She was two years older, olive-skinned, with long black hair, and any opportunity Henry got to stare at her unfettered, he took.

The girls were less afraid of water. In fact, they were wading out, in a line of four, into the surf, passing each progressive wave, leaping as they did, so the ocean broke as low on their bodies as they could handle, and it was because Henry was staring at Lani's back that he was the first one to see a stronger-than-anticipated wave crash across her chest and tear her bikini top clean off her body.

Lani shrieked, and shortly after Henry saw it, the other boys did, too: how she cupped her hands around her adolescent breasts and scanned the water around her for the stray top, which at that very moment was floating directly toward Henry and the boys.

"Grab it," one of the boys yelled, and Henry, quick as light then with those shortstop hands, was the first one to it. He scooped it out of the water, and the boys were cheering, since they had Lani now, could keep her top and force her to come out of the water to get it.

"Henry Gold," Lani said. "Help me."

Until then, Henry had not been sure she even knew his name. Henry took the top and began to move toward Lani. He went quickly, since he heard the boys behind him in disbelief about what he was going to do. He waded out to her with it above his head, and when he reached her, he demurely looked away and handed it to her, seeing out of the corner of his eyes how quickly and deftly she tied it on herself. She leaned down then and gave him a kiss.

"Thank you, Henry."

It was a feeling he would chase his whole life like a drug, her lips on his, the feeling of having made a pretty girl happy, and it didn't matter to him that when he reached the shore, Vince, the biggest of the kids, pushed him into the sand and held his face there with the bottom of his oversize teenage foot.

Now, in his living room and worlds away from that childhood, Henry picks up the phone. He stares at it for a moment and then presses his ex-wife Ruth's name. A moment later, she answers.

"Henry," Ruth says. "Everything okay?"

"Yes, of course."

"Okay."

"How are things there?" Henry asks.

"You sure everything is okay?" Ruth says.

"Positive. Look: I'm sorry to bother you. I'm going to Vermont tomorrow."

"Well, good for you, Henry."

"I'm hoping Jess can come with me."

"She has school tomorrow."

"Oh, right. I just thought it would be nice for her to be there when I open. She always liked that, remember?"

On the other end of the line, Henry hears Ruth sigh. "It's a school day," she says.

"Okay, right," Henry says. "Can I say hello to her?"

"She's asleep."

"Wow, what time is it?"

"It's almost ten. You sure you are okay?"

"Yes, yes, I'm fine. Today just got away from me, that's all."

Henry hangs up the phone and he can picture his nine-year-old daughter, in the house in Tarrytown that was once his. Jess is up in her room, in her single bed, sleeping, as always, on her back, her eyelids softly closed, the place he used to stare at when he would put her to bed, watching them flutter and flutter until they finally closed soft as pillows.

That night, Henry has a dream about Margot. In his dream, he returns to his apartment and goes into the bathroom, where the shower is on. Henry opens the door, and behind the glass is her form, and he smiles, as if it is what he expected, her here, in his place, or perhaps it is their place? For the bathroom is similar but different. The shower has a curtain, not the opaque glass that confronts him in the dream. He moves to the door and opens it, and there she is, no longer frozen in time as in so many of his thoughts and dreams about her she has been, but the age she is now, as he saw her today, her hair cut short, tiny crow's-feet emanating from the corners of her clear blue eyes.

Water is running off her shortish hair, down the width of her shoulders, across her breasts, and down the smooth table of her stomach. She smiles at him.

"Come in," she mouths to him, but she makes no sound.

"I love you," he says.

Margot just shakes her head, like she can't hear him.

"I love you," he says again.

Again, she shakes her head, and this time he yells it. "I love you."

That is all Henry remembers. In the morning, he wakes and walks across the street for a coffee and a bagel. The weather has held: a bright, beautiful, cloudless day.

An hour later, he is driving to Vermont, against the traffic, and this is a trip he has down pat, and by midafternoon, he is turning onto the narrow unmarked road that leads to his camp.

The road is what he fell in love with the first time. It rises quickly up, single-laned, through a pine forest that opens up into a broad meadow, wildflowers and tall grasses blowing slightly in the breeze. Then the road swoops down again into a deciduous forest, the sunlight dappling through the green leaves. And then, farther on, it opens once again and ends at a small clearing above a cliff, the lake in the distance. Parking here, he sees the roof of his cabin is slightly below the height of the cliff, and a staircase leads down to a second-floor entrance.

Henry gets to work. He moves the outside furniture, which has sat in the living room all winter, out to the deck. He opens the windows and airs out the mustiness. He plugs in the appliances and turns on the electricity. And then comes the arduous process of undoing what he did last fall, getting the water flowing out of the lake now and into the pump and filling the pipes into the house.

That night he grills a steak he bought at the general store and eats it with some lightly dressed spinach to feel virtuous, though it is only the steak he wants.

Henry eats outside at the table on the deck, drinking a bottle of cheap Rhône he also found at the general store, and while he eats he watches the sun fall behind the hills to the west, and the lake, rippling and glowing in the afternoon sun when he arrived, becomes as still as glass, a mirror full of trees, an Impressionist painting of the dying light.

Right before dusk, the resident loons arrive, the pair of them, back for the season. They glide in front of Henry's deck, as if he isn't there. It is their lake, after all. They are elegant swimmers. They dive under, and in the half-light of the fading evening, he can see their bodies underwater, like tiny dolphins, soaring, soaring and soaring, a calibrated dance, moving around each other as gracefully as acrobats.

Last summer, there was a baby loon. They would take turns teaching it to fish, each feeding it by catching a small pumpkinseed and swimming over to the baby with the squirming little fish clutched in his or her beak. Loons mate for life. You never see a loon alone. This year, the baby is gone. But how, Henry wonders, do they find each other? How do they choose?

Of course, he is not thinking about loons at all.

Things rise and things fall and sometimes they converge and sometimes they fall apart. The most one can hope for is that you find someone who can tolerate your flaws and your faults and see her way to loving you anyway. That maybe you figure out how to make a life together. That maybe you decide not to fight the darkness by yourself. The rest of it can only be a romantic notion, right?

It is the stuff of goddamn poets.

Margot, 2012

The cab is hot. It is suffocating. Henry's face, floating in front of her like a balloon, is gone. Margot is heading uptown. She rolls down the window, and the hot air that blows in on her doesn't help. How is it that he was suddenly there? Her fingers on the bird, soft, warm feathers rising one last time, the city loud as thunder around her, and there, in the only stillness for miles, stands Henry, resolute and fixed before moving toward her and saying her name.

Much earlier in her life, Margot was prone to panic. Mainly in her late twenties—a few episodes, nothing serious, though one time before her wedding she ended up in the hospital because her death appeared imminent. They strapped her to machines that, in defiance of all logic, said she was fine.

"You are having an anxiety attack," the ER doctor told her, as if he saw her kind several times a night. "There is nothing wrong with you."

Everything is wrong with me, she wanted to say, but didn't.

It is a failure that will compound throughout her life, a failure to speak her mind. But of course she knew that was only part of it. The harder thing to reconcile, always, is what she carries within her, the complications of the adult mind, the cognitive dissonance that allows for secrets and truths to reside next to one another and never emerge into the world.

Now, coming through Central Park, downslope through the trees and under the bridge, Margot begins to breathe again. The air is suddenly light and springlike, not of the city. The panic rising within her starts to recede, a familiar feeling to her, the sense that what was about to overwhelm her is then somehow falling away.

She can still feel the blood in her face, though, and in her mind is the image of Henry. He has aged well, for the most part, and is still boyish in his forties. Why did she run? Wouldn't the more appropriate thing have been simply to chat with him, old friends running into each other? Talk to him and then walk away. Wouldn't that have made it easier? Move into the teeth of the storm and hope it goes away. Of course, it is far more complicated than that.

This is the other thing Margot doesn't like about adulthood: Every interaction seems to bring with it a history, a context, and nothing is simple. Young children meet each other and after a moment of awkwardness play with ease. Adults circle each other like stray cats.

Last summer on the island, her daughter, Emma, had her

first boyfriend. One of those towheaded preppy boys who seem to grow like mushrooms after a rainfall on the island. The kind of boy who looks like he just stepped off a sailboat. He was tall and lean and sun-browned, the swoop of blond hair that covered his eyes a remaining semblance of awkward adolescence.

Watching them together, walking on the beach in front of their house, waiting until they were a reasonable distance away from her parents before holding hands, Margot was struck by the innocence of it all, the here and now of it, the impermanence of summer. Oh, she didn't want to know what they did out of sight, at night when they rode their bikes and hid on a blanket in the dunes. She had an idea, of course, and she trusts Emma, who has always been a cautious girl. But it's hard for Margot not to feel a twinge of envy in seeing her daughter experience things for the first time, those tentative first steps toward adulthood, when the days seem eternally long, and joy, simple joy, comes without strings or any depth of thought, as true as the salty breeze blowing off the sound.

The cab lets Margot off on Fifth, just across from the museum. A block away, at a coffee bar, Cricket is waiting for her. They have known each other their whole lives. They spent summers on the Vineyard, and attended the same schools from seventh grade through college. They both married men from similar families with similar ambitions: husbands who both work on the Street.

Until recently, Cricket lived in Darien, but with their only child at Trinity, they sold the house in Darien and moved into a new building in TriBeCa. Margot braces herself to hear about how great it is to live in the city, and how did ever they suffer for so long in the suburbs?

They exchange air kisses and Margot studies her best friend, put together in her Manhattan finest, of course, skinny jeans set off by a gold Hermès belt buckle, heels, and a frilly white blouse.

Before she leaves her to order a latte, Margot has this sudden idea that she barely knows Cricket, which of course cannot be true. She has known her longer than she has known anyone. Then again, she has had a similar feeling lately about Chad, her husband, waking up in the middle of the night and studying his sleeping face as if a stranger had somehow found his way into her bed.

Margot returns to the table, and the pitter-patter of small talk begins. The building, the building, the building. How great it is. How much they love it. Of course, Margot has never been there. This is one of the funny things about New York. Outside of major events, people keep their elegant houses to themselves. They meet in public spaces, the first floors of Manhattan.

Cricket moves on: Pilates class, and the new French restaurant that opened next door. The chef was somewhere else before; Cricket can't remember, but surely Margot knows, doesn't she? It was definitely in the *Times.*

As Cricket prattles on, Margot wonders when it was that they stopped really talking to each other. Margot means really talking. Confiding. At what age do women start speaking around each other?

After all, the woman across from her was once a young girl, a girl she used to bunk with at camp in the summer in the Maine woods, and when everyone else was asleep, they would climb into the same bed and whisper secrets back and forth, with the comfort of knowing that no two human beings could possibly trust each other more.

They have cried together over heartbreak. They have stood next to each other at each other's weddings. They have held each other's heads against the cold porcelain of the toilet after youthful nights of overindulgence. And now, somehow, having passed forty, they have grown armor, and the intimacy that defined their youth feels like it is gone forever.

Margot doesn't tell Cricket she ran into Henry Gold. She doesn't say that she can barely think because of it. She wants to tell someone how good he looked. He looked really good. He looked like Henry. And how that scared her even more.

Margot doesn't tell her she wonders sometimes if Chad is having an affair. That perhaps he is in love with someone younger than she, or is at least fucking someone, since God knows he barely attempts to fuck her anymore. Let alone come home before she is asleep.

Margot doesn't tell Cricket that she is painting and this makes her happy. Saying you are painting is almost like saying you are a painter, and what middle-aged woman has the hubris to do that when no one besides her husband has seen her work? Though is *happy* even the right word? Perhaps she simply doesn't remember what it is like to be happy, not that she's sad per se, but it's just that if there is anything she has learned, it is that there is no longer such a clear continuum as there was when they were younger, when she swerved from happy to sad with the synchronicity of a metronome. She dwells now in moments of gray.

Painting gives her pleasure, then, though pleasure is not the same as happiness. Pleasure is fleeting.

There are days, however, especially at the ocean, when she feels a surge of joy, and oftentimes her children, in certain singular moments and through the smallest of gestures—a glance, a smile, a laugh—allow Margot to see herself in them, to recognize that they exist only because of her, that they in fact are her, and this, too, can bring her back quickly to a place where she finds beauty.

But the truth is that some days Margot asks herself, Is this it? Is this all there is? Not that she would trade her life for anything. Despite the angst she sometimes feels, Margot knows how good she has it. Even Chad, who worries her, is never anything but kind. What else could she possibly want?

Though in Cricket's pretty brown eyes and her expensively dyed streaky blond hair, Margot sees a sadness reflecting back at her, a mirror of how she feels. And yet neither of them have the courage to acknowledge this truth. It is as if they have reached an age where that is no longer appropriate between friends. That's what therapists are for. Pay someone two hundred an hour to hear your problems. For everyone else, put on a good face. Let them know you are doing at least as well they are. And if you know bad things that are happening to other people, share them. It is the dark, satisfying pleasure of schadenfreude, and they are all guilty of it, whether they want to admit or not.

On the train home, Margot gets a text from Chad.

"Stuck here. Dinner with clients. How r u?"

"It's fine," she writes back. "I'm good."

That night she eats some leftover salmon with couscous and drinks a glass of white wine on the back patio. She stares out at the woods, beyond the formal gardens. Later, she wanders around her large, empty house, pausing at the kids' bedrooms, looking into them, thinking of both of them in their dorm rooms right now, her youngest certainly sitting at her desk for study hall and Alex doing who knows what. She thinks of Chad, in his tailored suit, at one of the steak houses he takes people, where they wheel the steaks out on carts that are bigger than your head. Chad holding court and passing around some ridiculously priced robust red wine made in small batches in a Sonoma garage, digging into his repertory of long-form off-color jokes, the men he is with guffawing with their heads kicked back when he eventually delivers, with a pitch-perfect timing developed over years, the biting punch line.

It's funny, Margot thinks, that wealth can give you lots of things, but one thing it often takes from you is family. The wealthy scatter like pollen in the wind, while the poor tend to stay together. Or is that even true? She doesn't know. What she does know is that her family now is no different from the one she grew up in. There is always this urge to keep moving. The world as playground, jumping from one spot to the next. Her father gone for months at a time for work in places like Singapore. She and her sister sent away to boarding schools as soon as they hit puberty. Her mother, at eighty, still not sitting still. As if by living so urgently, they can somehow separate themselves from the sadness of the masses.

In her bedroom, Margot props pillows up on her bed and climbs on it fully clothed. She puts her glass of wine on the end table next to her bed and picks up her iPad. And for the first time in about a year, Margot types the name Henry Gold into the search engine.

There he is on his NYU faculty page. The photo is black and white and clearly taken for a book jacket. The photo makes his black eyes pop even more than usual, and in them she can see that soft, gentle intelligence. He wears a dark jacket and a light shirt. His biography is to the right of the photo, and for probably the fifteenth time, she reads the third line of it. "His debut collection of poetry, *Margaret,* won the Yale Younger Poets prize."

Margaret, she thinks. Margot. Somewhere in her closet, buried, is a copy of the book, which she found used on Amazon years ago. She hid it in a shoe box in a place Chad would never look. On the cover is a picture of a woman, taken from behind, as she looks out a window. Margot devoured it the day it arrived, locking herself in the bathroom, her eyes filling with tears. Each poem is a moment, a day, she recognizes. Each poem is a whispered elegy to the two of them.

And the dedication in the beginning she knows by heart: *For you, wherever you are.*

Just from that alone, Margot thinks, I should have known he would never stop trying to find me.

Henry, 1991

Henry is in love. He is in love with this leafy upstate New York campus. He is in love with its brick buildings, with everything that is opening in front of him, his world suddenly as expansive as these rolling hills with their great glacial lakes, wide and cool and blue as the sky. The narrow streets of Providence, the triple-deckers and the gray, cracked asphalt, the clotheslines and antennas, have been replaced with impossibly green, impossibly wide-open spaces.

Baseball gave him this gift. Oh, he was a decent-enough high school student, good grades and well liked, but his test scores were nothing to write home about. He might as well have Christmas-treed the math test.

But he could really play shortstop. His senior year in high school, he wore a glove several sizes too small for him, and he did it deliberately so it would feel closest to his bare hand, and while a left-handed shortstop was so unorthodox as to be unheard of, he gobbled up every ball that came his way. As a hitter, he didn't have a ton of pop, but he could spray singles to all fields. By his senior year, Henry was all-city, and then all-state, and soon the bleachers were full of scouts.

The thing is, baseball loved Henry more than Henry loved baseball. His greatest strength as a young man might have been a preternatural sense of self-awareness. He was a marginal prospect and he knew it. The Boston Red Sox were not in his future. A bald old man chain-smoking unfiltered Camels told him this.

The man was a freelance scout, published some newsletter that was read widely. "I got you rated as average, slightly below on all tools," he told Henry after a high school game. "Except fielding. I gave you a seven out of ten. But you're a lefty playing shortstop, son. That's a nonstarter. Think about moving to the outfield," he said. "Put on some weight. You got good, fast hands. Maybe you'll grow into some power."

Other boys his age might have been angry about words so damning related to the thing one was most known for. But Henry was grateful for candor, and not surprised by it, for it supported his own assessment of where he was.

And so while there was still some talk about being drafted, it was the colleges he turned his attention to. At his request, his high school coach sent VHS tapes to coaches around New England and in New York and Pennsylvania. His mother was right, way back when she agreed to let him play organized ball. This game was going to open a door that would otherwise be closed to him.

And so Henry, in the fall of 1988, finds himself a student at Bannister College and the college's starting shortstop. As a Division III school, Bannister technically doesn't give scholarships, though one look at Henry's aid package would suggest otherwise. It is a wink and a nod.

The baseball coach sees Henry as a four-year star for his program, and has no idea that Henry is far more calculating than any eighteen-year-old athlete he has ever known. His aid package is for four years and, naturally, contains no mention of baseball.

Nevertheless, Henry does commit to playing his freshman year, and that spring he leads the team in hitting from the lead-off position, and plays a steady and sometimes spectacular shortstop.

All the things he always liked about baseball—those quiet moments before the ball was pitched, the anticipation of its being put in play, instincts taking over as he moved swiftly to his backhand position and scooped the ball with his small glove—are still true for him. He likes the crack of the bat. He likes watching the rotation of the ball as it streams toward him when he is at the plate, gauging in seconds whether or not to take the lumber off his shoulder and swing through it. It might be a beautiful, poetic game, but it is not a game often played by poets.

The other baseball players are not, to his surprise, his crowd. Like Henry, they are public school kids, rare here, and they are surprisingly local, most of them from nearby cities like Syracuse and Rochester, recruited like he was for their ability to hit or pitch or field. They are also more working-class than the student body as a whole, just like Henry, though none of them is Jewish, and this becomes a brief issue during fall practice, when the left fielder, a junior and a meathead, makes some joke under his breath about Hanukkah Henry.

"Excuse me?" Henry says.

"Nothing," the boy, whose name is Johnny, says. "Just messing with you."

Henry senses something in his posture, that he might actually be afraid of Henry, and doesn't expect the boy to challenge him. Henry tries something from the neighborhood then and says, "If there's a problem, maybe we can take a walk, figure it out."

"It's cool," Johnny says. "Relax, dude. Just busting your chops a little, you know?"

And Henry knows in that moment he has won something, though he also knows he hasn't come all this way just to live in Providence again. And maybe this is the beginning of the end of his baseball career, but it is also more than that, for Henry is changing.

The other baseball players do not live for words and ideas and language, which Henry increasingly does. A class on Latin American literature, taught by a pretty long-haired professor with a Spanish accent, introduces him to Neruda. Henry is enthralled by Neruda's story—his fame, reading poems in front of an entire stadium full of people. Henry loves Neruda's courage, the knowledge that his words and his poems will cost him his life and yet he marches on. Henry hadn't realized there were places in the world where poetry could have this kind of importance.

Mostly, though, Henry is drawn to what Neruda feels and what Neruda says and how he speaks of love. The poet talks of women in a way that channels Henry's own secret thoughts, but not the kinds of things he could ever say out loud in his old Providence neighborhood, or even here on this leafy campus, in front of the baseball team anyway.

Henry hadn't known men could talk about love this way. In reading Neruda, Henry sees the deepest part of himself, and he realizes he is not alone in thinking as he does, and it is then he decides he will be a poet.

It is an absurd idea. Who becomes a poet? People become bankers or lawyers, or go to med school and save lives. It is not something he can tell anyone about. His mother would be horrified. She was overjoyed when he got into Bannister and was able to go practically for free. She was overjoyed because she saw him becoming a lawyer or a doctor or working in some respectable profession where you wore a suit and went to work in an office every day, made plenty of money, and built a new life along the way. It was the idea that each generation is stronger than the one before. He would fulfill the promise of America her own parents had when they fled Poland half a century before. He would fulfill the promise of the name they'd given him.

At the beginning of his sophomore year, Henry does two things. The first is to declare his major as English. He tells his mother this is the fastest track to law school, and she smiles when he says it. She gives him a hug and says, "Oh, Henry," and he feels a little bad for deceiving her, but there will be plenty of time later to explain things.

The more difficult one is his baseball coach, whom Henry visits in his office in the basement of the athletic center. His coach is a hard man and Henry doesn't expect it to go well, and it doesn't. Coach is angry.

"My heart's not in it," Henry says.

"There's twenty-four other guys counting on you," his coach says, standing up and raising his voice. "Twenty-four guys, Henry, who all want to win a championship. What about them?"

Henry shrugs. "I'm sorry," he says.

"That's all you got?"

Henry thinks for a minute. "Yes," he says.

And so that semester, Henry signs up for his first creative writing class. There are twelve students around a wooden table in a small room with big windows that look out onto the main quad. The professor is a youngish man, a short story writer who recently graduated from Iowa, he tells them, as if this is important. He wears a uniform of tight jeans, cowboy boots, a white button-down shirt, and a tweed coat. His outfit never changes. His face shows a consistent four days of stubble. He insists everyone call him Jon.

The class is entry level and he assigns them prompts to write stories and poems. They are to write about childhood smells, that kind of thing. And then they bring them in and read them aloud to one another, and everyone critiques one another, with Jon moderating while tapping a pencil thoughtfully against his jaw, ensuring that nothing gets personal, which is no small task, since everything, for young writers, is by definition personal.

Henry loves the assignments, even the silly ones. He loves wrestling with the words and he loves playing with structure. Each poem is a tiny puzzle to be solved.

What he doesn't love is reading out loud in class. He is self-conscious about his voice, and especially his accent. He doesn't know anyone else with his accent at Bannister. People say to him immediately, "Where are you from? Boston?"

"Providence," he says.

Reading out loud, Henry thinks it is even worse. The effort to enunciate, to linger on each word, only makes it worse. The first time he reads, several of the girls giggle, and Jon shushes them. "Go on, Henry," he says, though Henry once again is reminded that he has traded being an outsider in one place for being an outsider in another.

Bannister is a particular college. For years, it had the reputation of being the most expensive undergraduate college in the country. Yet it is a step below elite. It is not Williams or Wesleyan. Once in class Jon tells them that Vonnegut used to teach here—before his time, of course—and famously described Bannister as catering to the moronic and dyslexic sons and daughters of the ruling class.

Henry laughs the hardest at this, and Jon says, "What do you think of that, Henry?"

Henry shrugs. "I'm not a moron and I'm not dyslexic and

I am certainly not from the ruling class, so it can't be true, right?"

Everyone laughs, and for the second time, Henry feels like maybe he has won something.

One fall afternoon, Jon stops Henry after his class and asks him to sit for a minute. Jon waits until the rest of the class filters out. Henry looks past him to a big maple outside that has already turned red, the color of fire.

"Do you like this class?" Jon asks.

Henry nods. "Very much. Why?"

"You're different from the others," Jon says, and Henry thinks he is talking about his background, his working-class voice devoid of *r*'s.

"Most of these students," Jon continues, "will take one of these classes, like some take a drawing class and never intend to become artists. You have that thing, though."

"'That thing'?"

"Talent, Henry. You can write. You hear language. Let me tell you a small secret."

Henry leans slightly forward. "Yes," he says.

"There are two reasons to teach writing, and neither of them is about teaching writing." Jon laughs. "You teach writing for a paycheck. That's first. Second, you teach writing to curate. Do you know what I mean by that?"

"I think so," says Henry.

"You curate by identifying students with talent. You then encourage them to keep going. In some ways, that's all you can do."

"I get it," Henry says.

"Keep going," Jon says. "If you want this, you can do it. Okay?"

Henry nods. "Thank you."

Walking out into the sunny afternoon, out onto the quad full of students sitting in small packs, dogs running wild, people throwing Frisbees, Henry feels better than he has in a long time. He realizes Jon has given him a gift, and though it will be a while before he realizes how important a gift it is, for Henry it is as if everything is suddenly different, smells different, looks different, and tastes different. He wants to take a bite out of all of it.

Margot, 1991

There was never a question that Margot would go anywhere but Bannister. Her father went to Bannister and her mother went to Bannister. Her sister, Katherine, graduated a year before Margaret arrives. Their parents met there. Her father is on the board. The field house that opened a few years before has his name on it: The Thomas W. Fuller Field House.

Her whole life, it seems, her parents took her to Bannister every fall for at least reunion, and with Cricket also choosing Bannister, Margot arrives on campus with a familiarity that most students do not have. There is a logical order to life that has been laid out for her, though Margot, unlike her sister, has chosen to question it every step of the way. She pushes against the strictures laid out for her. She tries to find the invisible walls that a girl of her station in life is not expected to walk into and she runs through them.

Some of it is just youthful acting out, the predictable behavior of a spirited girl who is the daughter of wealthy parents. At Stoneleigh-Burnham, a small school in western Massachusetts where all the girls boarded their own horses, she was expelled as a sophomore for literally letting the horses out of the barn during commencement, all those beautiful majestic Thoroughbreds, many of them more costly than four years of tuition, wandering around confused and startling the parents and grandparents of the graduates on a sunny day on the green.

A year later, she was sent home from a Swiss school for accepting in the mail a package of marijuana from a friend she knew from the Vineyard. Her parents sent her to an outdoor leadership program for wayward girls in Wyoming, half horse camp and half boot camp, and Margot got caught in the tent of a male instructor. He was fired and she was sent home three days in.

Once, the summer before college, her parents flew to New York for a dinner. Margot had the Jones boys over, as they were known, two brothers from her summer circle who both went to Deerfield during the year. With the house to themselves, they got into the liquor cabinet and into the fridge, and a few beers and a joint led to shots of tequila. Neither of the Jones boys really interested her—they were both handsome, although short—but Margot was drawn to their energy, their recklessness, and she was at an age when these things fueled her, the fierce intensity of now.

They were outside, behind the house, looking past the wild-crafted landscape to the open ocean. The sun was still summer-high in the sky, though the evening was coming on. The night was warm and there was little wind. Twenty feet off the beach was one of her father's prize toys, his Boston Whaler, which could sleep four.

"Dude," one of the Jones boys said, "that is such a sweet boat."

And as such things happen, that small germ quickly grew into a full-blown idea. There was a party the Jones boys knew about over on Nantucket, a bonfire out on the point of Madaket Beach, some thirty miles away, but that fast bitch, as one of the boys said, could get them there in about an hour.

"You know how to drive that thing?" Margot asked.

"Fuck yeah," the older of the two Jones boys said. "In my sleep."

And here was the beauty: the rippling blue-green ocean; the bright, warm sun; the big white boat cutting through the chop like a knife through warm butter, and the entire island becoming clearer behind them as it receded; Margot, sitting in the bow and pulling her cardigan around her against the wind while she looked back and saw the high bluffs of Aquinnah rising up like great sand castles to the sky.

At one point, the younger of the Jones boys, lighting another joint and bringing it around, first to Margot and then to his brother behind the wheel, said, "Dude, make sure you don't miss Nantucket, or we're heading all the way to Portugal."

The three of them laughed heartily at this, and Margot, high from the tequila and the grass, began to think that sounded pretty damn good, just pointing east and going and going until they ended up in another country. For a brief second, she entertained the idea of her parents' reaction when they saw the boat gone and it didn't return. There was something delicious in the idea of her father's anger, her mother's harsh disappointment, her sister, always so judgmental, saying "I told you so." But of course this was madness, as the boat had enough gas to get them to Nantucket and back certainly, but not much beyond.

And this, the inviting of trouble, suddenly nagged at Margot, a pin piercing the balloon of her good time, and she shouted to the Jones boys above the waves, "We can't stay long, you know. We have to be back before my mom and dad. Way before midnight."

"It's cool," the younger Jones said. "We'll make it work."

Out on the water, the sun was going down and the ocean was brilliant and the boat was fast as it steamed across the sound, Nantucket Island visible now, a hunk of brown in the early-evening light against the starboard horizon. To the right, a ferry chugged slowly toward the mainland, and out and about small fishing boats sat still as toys in the distance.

Soon they were approaching the island, and as it came into view, the younger Jones broke out the tequila again and they each did a shot, this time straight from the bottle. The boat slowed now and they followed the curve of the island from offshore, and they cheered when they saw Madaket and the fire they'd come for. It was suddenly dusk, grayish air where it used to be clear, and the younger said, "Dude, you know where the shoals are, right?"

"Yeah, man, I got this," his brother said, and a moment later, as if on cue, there was a sickening sound, like metal being sawed through, and then the whole boat lurched suddenly forward and Margot instinctively grasped the railing to stop herself from going over.

"What the hell, Jones?" she yelled, and now the sound they heard was at once overwhelming and wrenching and she wanted to cover her ears, but she was afraid to let go of the railing. Then another sound followed it, surprisingly congruent, a symphony that had suddenly reached its bridge, and now there was the sound of roaring water, as if somewhere below a thunderstorm had struck, a downpour falling off the side of a house invisible to her.

"Oh fuck," one of the Jones brothers said, and she didn't know which one and it didn't matter, for she had been at sea enough to know what this meant. The boat came to a complete halt and started, ever so slightly, to list to the left.

The engine was off and the three of them were looking over the side. In the growing dark, the shoal was clearly visible and the jagged rocks were right below the surface. Margot was too afraid to cry yet, but she knew the boat was sinking.

"What do we do?" she yelled. "What the fuck do we do?"

"We swim," said the older Jones.

Margot looked to the beach, maybe a quarter mile away. This was the craziest thing that had ever happened to her—her father's boat, which cost more than most houses, pierced in the hull and about to sink into the ocean off the coast of Nantucket. She had been in trouble before, but never like this.

They were young and fit and experienced swimmers from summer after summer on the island, so the swimming was the easy part. Swimming toward the beach shortly became like flying with the wind at their backs, pushing them in and in until they were walking with their soaking wet clothes in the high surf.

Turning around, they saw the dark had now fully crept in, and with the boat's running lights off now, it was if the Whaler had never been there, just the endless slap of the sea.

At the beach, the party was full of kids who moved in their circles; some of them Margot knew and some she didn't, but they were all kids from various boarding schools, versed in the same lingua franca. Once the incredulity died down, one of the boys who lived closest to the beach offered to give her a ride in his jeep back to his house so she could make the call she dreaded.

It was a practiced call and one Margot had made before. It was not her father she called, or her mother, though by making this call, she was in effect calling both of them.

Kiernan, her father's assistant, answered on the second ring. His strong South African accent was unwavering even as she told him most of the truth, skipping the tequila and the joints but otherwise keeping her account accurate. She knew that it was now out of her hands. And she also knew, from experience, that there was not much anyone could do to touch her.

In the end, as it is always does with the rich, propriety won out. Kiernan cleaned up the mess she'd made, as he was paid to, as he always cleaned up messes, she supposed. Discreet calls were made to the sheriff. No one wanted to make a fuss.

The boat was retrieved, repaired, and eventually replaced with a new one her father wanted even more. The Jones boys were temporarily banned from her house, and she was told she wouldn't be able to do all the things she usually did for the remainder of that summer, but after a week it was like it had never happened, with the exception of one conversation with her father a few weeks before she was set to depart for college.

This was on the Vineyard in August. The day was gray, with leaden skies, and cool for the season, the wind roaring off the sound and causing the American flag flying above the patio to wrap tightly around the pole and shake in the breeze. Margot's mother found her in her bedroom and told her that her father wanted to speak with her downstairs. Margot sighed but knew better than to protest: Her father, when he wasn't leaving the management of her to others, didn't ask for things, but expected them.

Her father was on the glassed-in porch, sitting in a white wicker chair, his face in profile as she approached, staring out at the endless gray sea. He wore a white polo shirt, tan chinos, and Top-Siders without socks. He turned to Margot when she reached him and gave her a half smile and motioned to the chair across from him. Margot sat down.

"I've been meaning to talk to you," her father said.

"About?"

"Bannister," her father replied. "It's coming right up."

"Two weeks," Margot said.

"Yes. I don't think I have ever said this to you before, or not like this. Between you and your sister, you are the one who is more like me, you know. You take risks. You have that spirit. That energy that can be your greatest strength or your greatest weakness, depending on how you use it. But the similarities between you and me when it comes to Bannister end there. You know what I mean?"

"I'm not sure," Margot said.

"Bannister wasn't a continuation of this life for me," her father says, using his hand now to sweep out around the room. "I didn't come into it with all the advantages you have. I was going there to kill it and I wasn't coming back. I decided I was going to hit the ground running on day one and never look over my shoulder. I knew what I wanted. For me, it was never about money. It was always about freedom."

Margot had heard this all before. How her grandfather had spent his life selling textiles to hotels and hotel chains, a job he was ill-suited for, and one that was unceremoniously taken away from him on his fiftieth birthday. How hard it had been for him to find other work and how her own father, at the time, sixteen years old, had worked three jobs to try to help them keep their small ranch house in Poughkeepsie,

New York, an effort that turned out to be in vain. How this life lesson had steeled him to become the man he would eventually be, et cetera, et cetera.

"I have always given you everything you have wanted. And I have tolerated, some would say to a fault, the mistakes you have made. But Bannister is different. It is the place that showed me the path to my own freedom. I have a lot of influence there, as you know. But this is your chance. This isn't high school anymore. You can't flunk out and have it be okay because there is another school. If it doesn't work out, your life will be very different, you know what I mean?"

Margot shrugged as her father's gaze lowered to her own eyes. "I think so," she said, just wanting this talk to end.

"Do you?" her father said. "Let me be clear. If it doesn't work there, if you make the wrong choices, your life will not be easy. You will have to find a way to support yourself. Some shitty job that means getting up really early in the morning. I know you think I won't do it, but I will. Do you understand now?"

Margot looked at her father. "I get it," she said.

His face softened. "Okay," he said. "It's going to be the time of your life. I would give anything to be there again."

Her father looked away from her then, back out to the sea and the leaden clouds. Margot rose to her feet, knowing she was dismissed.

And so Margot arrives at Bannister with her father's words echoing in the back of her mind. And for the first time, something clicks for her, and perhaps it is as simple as the fact that Bannister sits at the center of the many different concentric circles she already knows. She knows other freshmen from Vineyard summers. She knows others from boarding school, and still others from boarding schools that friends attended. Some she recognizes from New York. They are all no more than one degree of separation, it seems, and for a time, Margot moves with ease through that first year, surprising even herself by staying out of trouble, and perhaps it is the culture itself that allows her to do this, less of a college that first year and more one great extended party, classes, for her, something one must endure to get to the real action, the nighttime.

On campus, Margot is welcome everywhere, especially at the grand old fraternities that line the hill above the long, slender lake. Margot wraps herself in the social fabric of Bannister, rather than swim against it, and in phone calls home she can tell her parents are pleased with this, and for a time she does not care.

Margot gets the coveted invite to all the fall formals, nights when she and Cricket dress like grown-ups, and within the incongruence of frat houses, where the smell of stale beer and ratty furniture stands in contrast to the young students in their cocktail clothes, they move sideways through the crowds, practicing for the life of New York socialites that is their fate.

Margot finds a boyfriend—a sophomore named Danny, an attacker on the lacrosse team. He is a Theta Delta Chi, like her father was, and is square-jawed, stout, and fit, with a perfect head of curly hair. His nickname is "the Face," the result of an episode in which, during a game of pickup lacrosse on the quad, he was smiling at girls sitting and watching nearby rather than paying attention and completely missed a pass intended for the basket of his stick. It instead caught him square in the eye and he began to yell, "My face! My face!" It is also a nod to his obvious handsomeness and is only slightly ironic.

One night she arrives at Danny's frat house. She often spends the night here, since he has his own room and Margot shares one with a girl from Sri Lanka who never seems to leave the room other than for classes and has made it clear in her own passive-aggressive way that Margot is not to have anyone else in her bed.

As she comes through the main door, the familiar smell of beer and men hits her. She hears the sound of voices and the television in the large living room. A game is on. Margot comes into the room and a group of boys are on the couch watching football. Jeff, one of Danny's friends, nods to her and says, "Danny is in the poolroom."

"Thanks," Margot says. "Who's winning?"

"Giants, baby," one guy says.

Margot walks past them and into the large study, where the pool table is. It is dimly lit, and when she comes in, two figures are standing next to the pool table, Danny and a well-dressed man, tie askew, holding a pool cue in one hand, his other arm dangling around Danny's shoulder, talking closely to him. Her father.

It is a startling intrusion into her young life. Why is he here? How could he be here?

Danny and her father look up at the same time. Margot takes in the glasses of scotch on the rim of the table, half-empty, and the two of them smile at her as if this is an entirely normal occurrence.

"Here she is," her father says cheerfully.

"Dad, what are you doing here?"

"What does it look like?" her father says with a laugh. "Shooting some stick with my friend Danny here. Showing him how it's done."

Danny smiles that dimply smile. "Mr. Fuller refuses to let me win any games."

"Call me Tom, will you? Christ, we're brothers."

Margot holds it together to ask her father if she can talk to him alone, outside. Her father gives Danny this goofy smile and says, "Uh-oh," as if to say, I am in trouble now, and she hates him for it. She hates him for this whole thing, for tumbling into her life like this, at this moment when she is learning to fly and at a time when she has done exactly what he has asked.

For his part, Danny just gives her a look and shrugs and then goes back to considering the pool table, the lay of the balls scattered across the felt.

Outside, a waxing harvest moon casts a blanket of silver on the long lawn in front of the big brick house. In the half-light, she is struck again by how handsome her father is, his close-cropped gray hair and the line of his jaw and those feral pale eyes. All her life, Margot has heard this from her friends, how hot her father is, and she knows it is a big source of his power, what allows him to lead others the way he does, but also what allows him to bully his way through the world.

They stand close together, huddled like lovers. It is another of her father's techniques. He eliminates space to intimidate. Margot says again what she said inside. "What are you doing here?"

"I had a meeting with the president. Decided to stop by the house. I don't know what you're so upset about."

Margot is afraid she is going to cry. She doesn't want to. It is hard, this act of holding it all back, but the thing about fathers is that they have this ability to reduce one to an earlier state, to a time when a daughter first realizes her dad exists as a man in his own right, someone with a life that transcends her and her mother and the family. That there are lives he lives she knows nothing about. That he is capable of cruelty and people fear him.

"Hey, hey," her dad says. "Come on now."

Margot looks up at him and in the dark she bites her lip.

She grits her teeth and says, "Just go. Leave me alone. I have done everything you asked. Why do you have to be here?"

"Really?" her father says, grabbing her arm now. "I don't know what you are so upset about."

"What do you want me to do? You don't go here anymore. Why can't you just let me live my life?"

Her father's voice softens. "Listen, I'm proud of you. That's all. I'm going, okay? Just calm down, honey."

"Don't tell me to be calm," Margot says. "I don't want to be calm. And I don't need your approval."

And he tries to hug her then, puts his arms out, as if taking her into his arms can bridge the gulf that exists between them now. But Margot is not having it, not tonight. She does not want to hear about how he approves of Danny, how he has the stuff. She does not want to bend to his will, which everyone is used to doing.

"I'm leaving," Margot says, and she turns and walks away. She expects him to follow her, but he lets her go. And as she walks back to her dorm across manicured lawns freshly stiff with frost, Margot starts to cry and then she stops, and for a moment the tears make it hard to breathe and she wonders if anyone ever escapes.

Henry, 1991

Henry knows who Margot Fuller is. He knows her before he even sees her. In the weeks before freshman year started, he sat with the facebook they got in the mail, a booklet with head shots of each incoming first-year student. He is not alone in this, as the entire college will do the same when school opens, particularly the upperclassmen, perusing the faces of the new female students, categorizing them instantly and facilely as options or not.

Henry looks at the book for a different reason. He studies it like a mirror, looking for a reflection of himself. Sometimes he just stares at his own photo, his senior year in high school portrait, where he's wearing a corduroy jacket and his hair is long and curly, a toothy, lopsided grin on his face. *Henry Gold,* it says. Then underneath: *Providence, Rhode Island.*

For hours and hours, he pages through the booklet, studying the faces. He is the only one from Providence. Over and over the same towns appear. New York, New York; Darien, Connecticut; Greenwich, Connecticut; Rye, New York; Chestnut Hill, Massachusetts; Short Hills, New Jersey; Shaker Heights, Ohio; and so on.

The names of the towns themselves are meaningless to him. They are as exotic as Jakarta to his teenage mind, but part of him knows there is a reason for this narrow geographic reach, although he just doesn't yet know what it is.

And then there are the faces themselves. Almost exclusively white. There are pretty fair-haired girls after pretty fair-haired girls. And, of course, there is Margot. Margot Fuller, Darien, Connecticut.

Later, Henry will say that he lingered over her face more than the others. That something about her startling blue eyes, her brown shoulder-length hair, and her delicate nose with its slight upturn at the tip spoke to him. But this idea, his lingering on her, comes with wishful reflection, a glaring back through time that he himself doesn't fully trust.

In truth, freshman year, she is not someone he considers often. When it comes to the social hierarchy of Bannister, Margot is in an elite class. Even though she is only a first-year student, she moves in a pack of beautiful girls, Cricket and the two Whitneys, as they are known, both tall blondes.

Henry plays the wrong sport. No one cares about baseball. At games, a small smattering of fans sit on the hillside to watch him work his deft left-handed magic as shortstop. He has the wrong clothes and the wrong friends. He is invited to rush a few frats because he's an athlete, but he can barely afford to eat outside the cafeteria, so how could he possibly pay dues?

No, Henry is at the bottom with all the other freshman men, distinguished slightly perhaps by his athletic prowess. Though lacrosse is where the action is. Bannister is known for lacrosse. On Saturdays in the fall, the stadium fills, and lacrosse players are the one exception to the freshman rule. They move with impunity through the campus, regardless of their year.

For Henry, none of this surprises, for he expects to be on the outside. He makes a few friends. Painfully aware of the gift this education is, he never misses class. He studies. If he goes out, it is to the few big functions where no one will question his being there.

And while now and again he sees Margot Fuller around campus, it is not until they share a class that he really notices her. The class is a large one, a requirement for at least three different majors. European Intellectual History, it is called, a broad survey course held in one of the big lecture spaces, where the two professors stand below the students, who sit theater-style above, with their notebooks on small armchair desks.

Because of the clearly established social hierarchy of the school, Margot Fuller is not someone Henry would ever imagine talking to, or even having anything approaching an encounter with. But staring at her is a different matter altogether. She has a beauty that grows on him over time. Unlike her friends the two Whitneys, who are both blonde and symmetrical and far too conventional for him to find interesting, Margot has character in her face.

Her eyes are her most stunning feature, but it's more than that. There is a sadness in her face that belies how she has actually lived, or so Henry imagines, for how can he know how she has actually lived?

What he does know, after always arriving at that class just slightly on the side of tardy so he can choose a seat that affords him an unfettered view of her, is that Margot captivates him. While far below him a middle-aged professor with dark glasses on intones about Hume and Locke, Henry stares at Margot in profile two or three rows below him.

And one of the mysteries of the human brain is that someone can tell when they are being stared at. At one point, Henry is gazing at her dreamily when she turns and looks up at him. He is too slow to look away as quickly as he would have liked, and for the smallest of moments their eyes meet and he feels the blood rising into his face before he looks away casually, as if he was just absentmindedly scanning the room.

By his sophomore year, Henry has found an unlikely home at the college, among the theater people and the aspiring writers and the artists, the ones who eschew the fraternity scene for a small, dimly lit downtown bar. At night, they meet at the bar, with its upholstered booths, and drink bourbon with ginger ale and talk about novels and poetry and movies. They are conversations he has never imagined having before, certainly not in Providence, and within him he feels this great swell of change, aware that he is becoming something new.

And even as the fall turns to winter and the leaves fall off the trees and the wind that blows off the lake is icy cold and he has to pull his long coat around him against it, he has around him this sense of the possible that in the past he always associated with spring and the start of baseball.

That winter, he has his first real girlfriend, a skinny, dark-haired aspiring actor named Sue. Henry cannot tell if he loves her or not. She is part of his new extended crowd, and he likes it when she sits next to him at the bar, snuggling slightly into him, and he likes how she seems to listen more appreciatively when he talks, as if his words are fat with importance. He is grateful to her on those nights when they lie in his small single dorm room and make love, the way her hair falls down around her face when she is top of him, the soft kindness of her hands on him. Sue gives Henry, for the first time, the sense of how eternal and lovely life can be, slow and patient, and after they make love, he feels this rush of energy come over him and he wants to talk and write and make poetry in front of her. Sometimes he gets out of bed and it is deep in the middle of the night and under slight lamplight he reads to her the things he has written that day. He loves how she listens, her head cocked, looking away from him to the wall, nodding when a particular phrase hits her ear like a song.

But sometimes Henry misses being alone in a way that reminds him he has been alone his whole life. It is the fate of only children to learn how to be alone, to learn how to desire it. And now and again he asks Sue if he can take a night off, and he can see this idea bothers her. And then once she wants to smoke a joint and they do, in his room, and after they make love and he is particularly attuned to her slender body, the barely visible rise of her breasts, and it is as if he disappears into the pieces of her without seeing the whole, and this doesn't disconcert him until afterward, while they are lying next to each other, starting up at the ceiling, when she says, "Henry, do you love me?"

Henry considers this. He doesn't even know what it means. He knows what it means to love his mother, and to love his quiet, simple father, and that is a love that never really has to be spoken or imagined; it just is. Henry enjoys Sue and sometimes he misses her when she is gone. He has gotten jealous when she leans in close to one of his friends, and there is an easy sexuality about her, a comfort with herself that she projects out into the world. But if she left tomorrow, would he be okay? Is this the standard? Could he live without her?

And in the moment she asks him this, Henry decides that yes, he could, and he responds honestly.

"I don't know," he says.

"You don't know?"

Henry turns and looks at her brown eyes and he can see that he has hurt her. "I'm sorry, I don't know."

"That's a weird fucking answer," Sue says.

"What do you want me to say?"

"I'd rather you'd said no," says Sue, and with that she is standing up, slipping into her jeans and buttoning her shirt.

"Wait," Henry says, but he doesn't mean it. He wants her

to go. He wants her to go as a test to see how it feels, to try on her angry absence like a coat he covers his shoulders with against the cold.

And with that, she walks out into the winter night. A few days later, they are together again. But it has changed. When spring comes, they have simply drifted apart like the ice on the lake.

By the end of that year, Henry has become the darling of the English Department. All the professors know him by name, and he loads up on creative writing classes. They start treating him almost like a peer, at least to Henry's idea of what that might mean, choosing him and a senior girl to attend dinners with visiting writers. Many of them suggest he call them by their first names, and one of his professors, a kind-eyed, matronly gray-haired woman who wears long, flowing dresses, tells him to call her Deborah before she says to him one day in the long hallway outside the faculty offices, "Henry, you need to decide what kind of poet you want to be."

"What do you mean?"

She smiles at him. "It's your next step. You are a poet. You do know that?"

"I think so," he says.

"You can be a great one," she says.

Henry blushes. "Thanks."

"But your next job is to decide what you want to be. To find your own voice. The one that speaks honestly to the world."

"I'm not sure I like my voice very much," Henry says.

Deborah arches an eyebrow. "I don't understand."

"Listen to me," Henry says. "The way I talk. No one else here talks like that."

Deborah smiles broadly. "Yes," she says. "This is what you must write about."

"How I talk?"

"No, no. But yes. Where you are from."

"No one wants to read about the West End of Providence," says Henry.

"Oh, I disagree," Deborah says. "Tell the raw truth of things and everyone will want to hear what you say."

That night, Henry stays away from the bar. He holes up in his room with the window open and the warm spring air coming off the lake. He makes a pot of coffee on the little hot plate he has and sits at his desk, and he writes differently from the way he ever has before. He lets the poems fall out of him, telling himself not to self-edit, just let them find the page.

He writes about his mother and her black clothes and her black eyes and her fierceness. He writes about his father, who can sit silently in a room after a day of cleaning floors and yet never let anyone into his thoughts. He talks about the blue streets of his neighborhood slick with rain. He writes of the clotheslines and the antennas and the peeling paint. He writes of his shame about being the only Jew for blocks and blocks, of trying to mask it by learning how to bat a ball. He tells of those summer trips to Vermont, the only place he ever felt like himself. He describes the sound of his father's oar slipping into inky water, the whir of the fishing reel as it unspooled, of hearing birds for the first time.

When Henry finally puts his pencil down, he has filled ten pieces of paper. He loves the look of them, the poems, how they sit in the middle of the page with all that white around them, cabins in the snow.

Outside, the first colors of dawn are above the lake. He is exhausted but elated. It is like the moment after a virus leaves the body, the catharsis that comes with departure.

Later that day, he rushes to Deborah's office and thrusts the stack of poems at her. "Look," he says.

"Henry," she says. "Slow down."

"Sorry," he says.

But while he sits there, she takes the pages in her hands, slides her reading glasses onto the edge of her nose, and he can tell from the look on her face that he has something special. A few weeks later, she tells Henry that a very famous poet will be coming to speak and she would like Henry to read before he does, in front of a large audience of faculty and students.

"Are you serious?" he says.

"Yes," she says. "The Providence poems. Read three of those."

The reading is in the college's black box theater, a room that holds three hundred in stadium seating. In the days leading up to it, Henry cannot get the image out of his mind of the sea of faces above him, hundreds of eyes, a spotlight on him. Hours before, he feels like he might he throw up, and pacing around his small room, practicing, Henry begins to think of excuses he could make—a sudden flu, a death in the family, anything to get out of it.

But he wills himself to take the walk across the campus. The night is warm and the quad is full of students lounging about, and some people he knows greet him along the way, but if anyone knows he is about to take the biggest leap of his life, they do not say anything to him.

The theater is already starting to fill up, and as he comes in, Deborah spies him from the stage and motions to him. He goes to her, and she says, "There is someone I want you to meet."

In a fog of anxiety, Henry goes up onto the stage and then past the thick curtains to the area behind. The famous poet is standing there, next to a small table with a bottle of wine and glasses on it. He is not what Henry expects; in fact, he looks to Henry like a banker or a corporate titan. He wears a navy blue suit and a red tie, and he is clean-shaven, with short-cropped gray hair and horn-rimmed glasses. When he smiles, his face is as deeply lined as tree bark.

"This is Henry," Deborah says, "the student poet I was telling you about."

"Henry," the famous poet says. "I have heard good things about you." And then, looking at Henry's face, his tight expression, he says, "Here, have a glass of wine. It helps. Trust me."

Henry takes the wine and sips it. He has drunk wine only a few times before and to him it tastes like sour apples. Beyond the curtain, they can hear the room filling up, and the poet asks Henry a few questions, which Henry somehow manages to answer, and then the poet says, "Where you from, kid? Southie? Charlestown?"

"Providence," Henry says.

"Listen," the poet says. "Is there a girl you like? Someone you want to impress?"

For some reason, Henry thinks of Margot Fuller, and he can suddenly picture her, and this serves only to terrify him more. "Sure," says Henry.

"Think she'll be here tonight?"

"I don't know."

"Well, it doesn't matter. But if she is, just read to her. And if she isn't, just read to her, you know what I mean? And be patient. Nothing is more important to women than patience. You will learn this," the poet says, and then he laughs. "Be patient. Because when you are patient, you will be slow. And then you will dwell on each word and everyone in the room will feel your poetry."

Henry nods. He does not know what to say to this, so he just stands there nodding, and he finally says, "Thank you."

Ten minutes later, it is like a dream, hearing Deborah's voice echoing through the theater, then her words stopping and his slow walk to the podium, looking up and seeing the faces arrayed in front of him, the air warm and thick with the number of people inside.

Henry is happy for the podium, this small wall between him and them, and his hands shake as he lays the paper down, and he can feel the muscles in his legs contracting and flexing, as if his knees have been tapped with a rubber mallet.

"'Mother at Home,'" he says, reading the title, and there is a slight giggle in the crowd in front of him, and he knows it is because of how he says *Mother,* coming out in his accent more like *Mutha.*

But then he is reading, and he reminds himself to look up from the page, and there, halfway up in the crowd, Margot Fuller looks back at him and he remembers the advice of the famous poet. He stares down at the white paper in front of him and now he imagines each word as a single, separate thing, and he reminds himself to be patient, to hold each word like he would a baseball in his hand. And when he looks up in that moment after the first poem and before he launches into the second, the crowd has shrunk to an audience of one.

Margot, 2012

During the second week of June, the night before Chad is set to leave for a conference in New Orleans, Margot and her husband have dinner out at the one bistro on Main Street anyone goes to. They order drinks, and with their menus in front of them, they sit in silence for a while. Looking around the room, Margot sees other couples sitting in silence and she thinks, This is what marriage is. There comes a time when you just don't have much to say to each other anymore. There is no one to impress and the things you share, the children, are no longer here.

To make conversation, Margot says, "Isn't it going to be hot down there?"

"I checked earlier," Chad says. "It's like a swamp."

"Why don't they do these things in January, when people actually want to be in a place like New Orleans?"

Chad smiles. "Because it's cheap."

"It seems like an odd way to save money," Margot says.

Margot looks around. A few tables away, a younger couple are deeply engaged with each other, both leaning in and making the table smaller. She has a pang of memory. They used to do this, too, when they were first together, Saturday nights when they ate out in the city and the room disappeared around them, and then after they would walk back to his apartment and make love and then stay in bed the entire next day, sharing a copy of the *Times* and then watching movies curled up next to each other until the night came again.

"You should come with me," Chad says all of a sudden.

"Where?"

"New Orleans," he says. "I have some downtime." He smiles. "Staying right in the French Quarter. We could find some trouble, I bet. What do you think?"

Margot smiles. He is making an effort, though it is a half-hearted one, since he knows she will treat his question as rhetorical, and for a moment she considers surprising him and saying she will go, just to see how much it throws him off. But Chad is too good at all of this for her to do that. Plus, she doesn't want to. She doesn't want to be on a plane, and the idea of New Orleans saddens her. She imagines waiting for him all day in an air-conditioned hotel room, looking through half-parted curtains to the street.

In the morning, she watches Chad ready himself, come out of the bathroom fully dressed—when did they become so modest? And a moment later, he is bending down and giving her a kiss on the forehead, and then he is out their bedroom door with his garment bag slung over his shoulder.

Margot falls back asleep. When she wakes, it is past nine. Downstairs, she makes coffee and rummages around the fridge until she finds some yogurt. She eats halfheartedly, and looking out the window to the expanse of lawn in the back, she can see that it is a stunning day. Bright sun. For some reason, this energizes her, and she gets an easel and her paints and then she is outside, the sun on her face, mixing oils on her palette, loving the way they swirl together and become something entirely new, and then the rough physicality of applying the paint to the blank canvas, pushing the color into all that white, the unconscious beauty of her mind and her hand coming together and leaving the rest of her out of it.

Painting, for Margot, is like leading a secret life, and an hour later when she steps back and looks at what she has done, an abstract representation of the world outside her house, it is as if she has taken what she can see and shaken it up in a snow globe so that she is the only one who can possibly discern what it used to be, and this feeling both pleases and elates her.

But now with that work done, Margot is feeling suddenly unmoored and restless. It is not as if Chad hasn't gone away before—he travels a lot—it is something else. She paces around for a while and out loud she says to herself, "Fuck it." And shortly thereafter, she is burning down the Merritt in her Mercedes SUV toward the city, and there is something about the impulsivity of it all, hastily taking a shower and packing a bag and driving into New York, that both thrills and frightens her.

On West Seventy-ninth Street, she checks into the Lucerne Hotel, a terra-cotta and brick building on the corner of Amsterdam. It is not a place she has stayed before; in fact, it's a little boutiquey for her general taste, but she has eaten at the restaurant attached and she wants to stay there precisely for the reason that is not the kind of place they usually stay. Chad always wants to be downtown, some homage to youth. The Upper West Side is for old people.

Margot rides the elevator upstairs to a sixth-floor room with a marginal view out to Amsterdam Avenue. She puts her overnight bag down and almost instinctually lies down on the bed. The ceiling is high and a chandelier hangs down. Otherwise, the room is small. She wonders if maybe she can nap but decides she cannot and looks at the clock. It is just past one.

Margot rises and from her bag takes a baseball hat and a pair of sunglasses. She is wearing jeans and flats and a T-shirt. She pulls her hair into a ponytail and slips the hat on and pulls it down.

Out on the street, she moves into the midday crowd. Women pushing strollers and a group of Hasidic men with their black suits and their curls tumbling down the sides of their faces stand at the corner, waiting to cross. A police car sits parked on Seventy-ninth, two female officers inside. Young German men wait for a cab, wearing skinny jeans and shiny, pointy brown shoes. Four of them with the same haircut, all dark-haired, each shaved tight on the side and then a long lock hanging over their foreheads. They speak in rapid German and photograph everything. Margot feels old.

This is madness, she thinks. What is she doing? The anxiety suddenly rises inside her. Standing in front of the hotel, she wonders if she wears it on her face. She takes out her sunglasses and puts them on.

Margot begins to walk. She heads north up Amsterdam, past the row of bars, and even during midday the outdoor tables are generally full, young people, mostly, drinking beer behind iron fences. No one pays her any attention, and this is one of the beauties of the city: It takes a lot to stand out. She knows people in this neighborhood, of course, and that is a concern, though most of them are closer to the park. And anyway, she had an appointment, right? That is what she will say.

At Ninety-second Street, Margot takes a left and heads toward the river. Partway down the block, she begins to check numbers. She found his address by Googling him, and a donation to a political campaign showed up. There were other Henry Golds, but this address made sense to her. It is not far from Columbus Circle, where she last saw him. Plus, it is the kind of place where a poet of Henry's age would live.

The building, when she finds it, is nondescript, seventeen stories or so and without any defining characteristics. One of those New York buildings that no one who doesn't live there will ever consider twice.

Margot suddenly realizes she is the only one on the block. She looks toward Broadway and then up toward Amsterdam.

What if Henry were to walk out right now? They would be face-to-face.

She quickly retreats across the street. Fifty feet away sits a bench, and Margot goes to it and sits down. She hadn't thought this through very well, she decides. She pulls her hat down a little tighter and looks nervously up and down the street. She wishes suddenly she had a newspaper, as in the movies. Someone doing a stakeout like this always has a newspaper. She reaches into her pocket and takes out her phone, and this is what she will be doing if Henry comes down the street. She will hide into her phone.

Margot sits on the bench, and for a while nothing happens. A few people stroll by. An elderly black man pushing a shopping cart asks her for change, but she tells him she doesn't carry any, and he moves on. Chad texts her to say he has landed and that it's a good thing she didn't come. The air is like soup down there, he says.

Margot instantly writes him back and says she is glad he made it safely. The day is warm, but where she sits is shaded. She keeps thinking she should just get up and go back to the hotel and call this foolish thing off, but she cannot will herself to move. At one point, a woman of about her age goes into the building, and Margot studies her from a distance and wonders if it is Henry's wife. It occurs to her that she has been assuming for some reason he is not married, when in fact she has no idea what his situation is. For all she knows, he lives in this building with his wife and kids. Perhaps he is perfectly happy. This is indeed stupid, she thinks, and she is about to rise and walk back to the hotel, check out and get in her car and drive back to Darien, when she sees him.

Henry is coming toward her, but thankfully on the other side of the street. Margot's heart rises as she watches him stroll, a messenger bag slung over his shoulder, his button-down shirt rolled up at the sleeves, every bit the professor. She looks down at her phone as he gets closer to her but then peers up at him, praying that he will not look across the street and see her on the bench. But he walks with that practiced city weariness, looking straight ahead, not so much as glancing across to where she sits.

A moment later, he disappears into the building. Margot scans up the facade, though she doesn't know what she is looking for. If it had been night, perhaps a light would come on, though it would be too far up for her to see anything anyway. She counts the stories. She knows he is in 14C, though she doesn't know which way his apartment might face. When she reaches the fourteenth floor with her eyes, she lingers there, as if those implacable windows might reveal something.

Margot sits there for a while. There is more foot traffic now, since it's the end of the workday, people returning home from downtown offices. No one pays her any attention at all. She tries to imagine Henry inside, perhaps pouring himself a glass of wine, perhaps staring out the window at a slice of late-afternoon sky. And in that moment, Margot thinks she really should leave, but as she thinks it, she also feels more alone than she ever has in her life. Where should she go? Should she go back to the small hotel room with its chandelier and windows that don't open? Back to her empty house in Darien to pace around its large rooms and stare out at all the features, the shrubbery, the lawns, the gardens, that separate her from the rest of the world?

Margot wills herself off the bench and crosses the street. Her heart is racing. She is a teenager again. This is insane. Oh, she wishes she had a drink, but she tells herself just to move forward. Keep going and don't think.

She reaches the building, Henry's building. There is no doorman. Looking through the glass, she sees that the lobby is empty. She tries the door and it is locked, of course. Next to her is the row of buttons that buzz each apartment, many of them with names next to them, some without. His, of course, is without.

That instant before she presses down on 14C feels like a lifetime. She is going to do it. She is not going to do it. She must do it. There is no choice. Oh, how could she? What is she about to do?

And then she does. She holds it down. She hears the long, rewarding buzz and she tells herself, It's okay, I will hear his voice and say I pressed the wrong button. He will not recognize my voice after all these years, will he?

But there is no answer. She holds it down again, this time longer. She imagines the loud buzzer echoing through his apartment, Henry putting down his glass of wine and moving to the door. She holds it down the third time and this time she doesn't want to let go, and now she wants him to answer even if she might not be able to speak in return, but there is no voice coming over the intercom asking who it is; there is no sound of the door in front of her releasing its lock, only the abject silence of a uncaring stone building and the sound of a garbage truck moving down the street behind her.

Henry, 2012

Henry's heart, this day, is not in the classroom. Through the tall windows of his classroom, the early summer sun streams in, and he opens the windows before his workshop students arrive, something he rarely does, since the sounds of the street are not exactly conducive to focusing on the poems in front of him.

He muddles through his two workshops. Even Ricky, a young black poet from Queens who reminds Henry of a young Henry, all raw talent and earnestness, cannot fully get his attention. But when you have been teaching for as long as he has, you become skilled at fudging it, knowing when you need to tune in, what comments you can use to swiftly redirect a debate that has gotten stale, or, more damaging to the psyche of the young writer, personal.

In the weeks since he saw Margot outside the Time Warner Center, it is as if he has been in a state of suspended animation.

Henry goes through the motions of the day, and that afternoon, riding the crowded subway uptown, he sees a woman in profile in the reflection of the glass, and he turns, half expecting it to be her. And, of course, it is not. But seeing her opens the possibility for him that it will happen again, and at the very moment he least expects it. He moves through the world both heightened and aware and also resigned to the fact that it was pure chance, a moment in time certain not to repeat.

Back in his building, Henry waits for the elevator, and when it opens, his neighbor Russell Hurley is there in his workout clothes, riding up from the basement. Russell recently remarried, a woman named Betsy, though for a time the two of them were the token bachelors in the building and struck up a friendship. Russell works in the DA's office, and once and a while they used to get together for a beer and watch a game, though that was when Russell was single. Now Henry barely sees him anymore.

Russell is an ex-jock as well, a college basketball star, and stands half a foot taller than Henry. In the elevator, Russell greets him enthusiastically, and Henry is immediately reminded of how long it is has been since he has worked out, since he has broken a sweat, and for a minute he feels the guilt of his inactivity.

"Hey, man," Russell says. "How have you been?"

"Crazy busy," Henry says, though this is not really true.

"I know it," Russell says.

For a moment, they stand in silence as the elevator ticks upward slowly. Russell breaks the silence by saying, "Hey, what are you doing now? Come over for a beer. Betsy brought this stuff back from Vermont. Heady something. I guess it's a big deal in the beer world."

It is the last thing Henry wants to do after today. Mostly, he wants to be alone with his thoughts, perhaps stare out the window and maybe, for the first time in months, put pen to paper. He wants to start a poem. Not finish one, because that would be too much to ask. But to write again, that he can imagine, that feeling of the blood coursing through his veins.

But Henry has always had a hard time saying no, and today is no different, so he finds himself telling Russell that would be great, let him just drop his bag off and he'll be right over.

"Perfect," says Russell.

And in the hallway, they split up, and in his apartment Henry hangs his messenger bag on one of the kitchen chairs and then is back out into the hallway when he hears the buzzer. Henry stops. It goes off again. He considers turning around and going in to answer it but then decides it couldn't be his place; he never gets any visitors and he is not expecting a package. No, he thinks, hearing it again, it must be coming from 14A, where Mrs. Goldstein lives. Henry continues down the narrow hallway to Russell's and leaves the incessant ringing behind.

Margot, 1991

"He's adorable," Margot whispers to Cricket in the large auditorium. They are required to be there, an elective both of them are taking on American literature, one of those survey classes with a famously easy professor. If they went to the reading, he would eliminate one paper.

"Who?" Cricket whispers back.

"The poet boy, look at him."

"I think you're losing it."

"He's adorable," Margot says. "The accent. Those eyes. And the words. Listen to the words."

"You're really losing it," Cricket says.

Outside, the spring night is warm and the sun has set over the low hills, but traces of it, long, slender ribbons of purple and red, are visible above the trees. They wait for him. Students stream out of the theater and walk past the two of them, and when the building is almost empty, there is Henry by himself, walking out and staring around as if it is odd to be outside.

Margot stands back while Cricket approaches him. She witnesses their conversation, sees Henry look up in her direction, and she tries to read his expression. Is it fear? Shyness? Is it a lack of interest?

A moment later, he makes the short walk with Cricket over to where she stands.

"Hi," Margot says.

"Hello," he says, and it is almost as if he cannot look at her, his dark eyes glancing at her face before moving away. Margot finds it rather endearing.

"I loved your reading," she says, and it's true, she did; it moved her, his words, and it is because she had never heard anyone be so honest about anything before. She had never heard a man talk about women that way. She had never heard a man confess to a profound love and, at the same time, deep embarrassment in the presence of his own mother. It seems to Margot that when reading, Henry was all exposed heart, and listening through the veil of his thick accent and the rise and tumble of his incantatory language, she felt like he was speaking directly to her.

"Thank you," Henry says. Then: "I was nervous."

"It didn't show."

"No? I was shitting bricks. Excuse me, I didn't mean to say that."

"It's okay," she says, laughing.

Margot knows by looking at him that she will have to

lead. It is not something that she is used to, and if someone had asked her before this evening if the idea even interested her, she would have said no. But Henry's words suggest fragility, and she thinks maybe this extends to who he is, but she can also sense his strength, hidden somewhere like a secret, and this is the part she wants to know.

"Walk with me," she says.

And like that, Cricket just recedes into the distance with a thin wave, and the two of them take off across campus. Henry is taller up close than he looked onstage, and as they walk, first across the quad and then through a break in the old red stone buildings and toward the lake, the only logical outcome when she thinks about it, she senses that he is happy to be moving, that it is relaxing him.

They come up a final rise and in front of them is the main street that runs along campus and beyond that is the broad expanse of lake, a mile across here, inky black in the exhausted light and stretching out of view on either side, a giant finger cut into the earth. All along here, benches have been placed to capture the view of the open water, and on this warm night many of them are taken by couples, so without talking about it they move along them until they find one that is open.

"Should we sit?" Margot says.

"Sure," says Henry.

On the bench they can sit side by side and look out and not have to look directly at each other, though Margot looks at him more than he looks at her, and she knows this is his shyness and she does not mind. When she does look at Henry, it is his long lashes she notices and the way his mouth purses when she asks him a question and then how a moment later it relaxes. They talk about the reading. Henry tells her how he fell in love with poetry. "I want to be a poet," he says.

"You are a poet," she says.

"Not yet." He laughs. "Not the kind of poet I want to be."

And this, Margot decides, more than his handsome earnestness, his long lashes and his warm, dark eyes, is what draws her to him. It is the first time she has met a boy here who knows what he wants to do with his life with great certainty, and the thing he wants to do is not go work for his dad's firm, or just figure it out in New York, or even, like Danny, know that for the rest of his life work or not work will always be an option. It is not something Margot has ever really considered before, but it is his raw ambition that draws her in, the impracticality of it all, this idea that he wants to do great things with words, that he wants to chase some kind of ancient fame, perhaps even become one of the people they read about in books. It is something she wishes sometimes that she had, instead of always making light of her love of painting if anyone asks, as if it could only possibly be a hobby and not something ever carefully considered.

And sitting on that bench, looking out at the lake, she knows tonight she will kiss him and soon that she will sleep with him and she also knows, more broadly, that if she doesn't want to fall in love with him, she needs to decide that now.

Margot turns toward Henry and she doesn't say anything.

He is aware of her staring at him, and in a moment he turns toward her. Her face is upturned and a few people walk by in front of them, shadows in the night, and Henry quickly glances toward them and then back to her, and when he does, he leans forward and brings his lips to hers and then they are into it.

Henry, 1991

"I want to watch you write," Margot says.

"It's not very interesting," says Henry. "Watching someone write."

"Well, I think it is."

"It's not like baseball."

"Baseball is boring."

"Bite your wicked tongue," Henry says, and laughs.

They are in his room. It is warm and the windows are open and it is late. Now and again, the voices of students coming loudly back from the bars drift up to them. Henry lies on the bed naked and spent after making love. Margot is walking around the room, wearing this fedora he bought for himself on a lark. She is wearing only the fedora. She is magnificent. All of her is magnificent. The rise of her small breasts, the way her hair falls gently over her face. He loves the very shape of her, the wondrous curve of her hip. How she moves, strong and feral and magnificent to him. How each part of her comes together into a coherent whole: the perfect poem.

Henry is in love. He is in crazy, mad, nutty, insane love. He thinks of nothing else but Margot. The rest of the world is something that happens outside these walls. Margot is something that happens only to him. Margot is something that could happen only to him.

It has only been two weeks since they met, but it feels so much longer, lifetimes together. Did he have a life before her?

Henry has to remind himself to breathe sometimes. He has to remind himself that is okay to not be with her every single moment. He has to remind himself that she will still be there if he goes to class by himself.

That spring, Henry moves through his days with an electric urgency. Everything he sees is throbbing, alive, bright. A mania overtakes him in such a way that he wonders if he has been asleep for all his years and this is what it feels like to finally wake up. As for sleep, he barely needs it. In the mornings, he wakes with the sun and always before Margot, and this is when he writes. The words pour out of him in great jumbles that he seeks to tame on the page. Henry loves words. He loves how they fall off his tongue, like syrup spiraling off a spoon. He loves the music of words, the math of them, the logic of shifting them around like numbers until they make just the right sound. Mostly, though, Henry loves that words allow him to organize the world around him, to make order out of chaos, to take life and family and in short phrases bend them into something as pure as a baseball diamond on a summer evening. Words are a way to make sense of it all.

There is no friction between them. There is no awkwardness. It's instantly easy, almost too easy, though there is one exception. Until now, they have moved in different circles, Margot with her elite group, the pretty girls and the lacrosse players with the large fraternity houses as their anchor. Henry, by contrast, has become part of the underground of artists and actors and musicians who gather at the little dive bar and have made it their own.

And Henry and Margot don't speak about it, but they both intuitively understand that he cannot move into her universe with the same ease that she can move into his. So for a few nights he takes her out and introduces her around, and Henry sees the reaction from some of his crowd, and he knows it is not lost on her, either, the idea that Henry Gold is seeing Margot Fucking Fuller, of all people. And mostly he doesn't care, but once he overhears his friend Drew make a whispered comment about Margot to the others.

Drew is the one who Henry wanted to be when he first joined this crowd. Drew is an actor and the best one among the bunch of them, always playing the lead in contemporary versions of Shakespeare, where the actors, thanks to a particular fetish of the theater director, are dressed in Vietnam-era clothing. Drew has long dark hair that hangs to his shoulders and wears a small stud in one ear.

One night after Drew mutters something under his breath

about troglodytes, his new favorite word, and one he uses all the time now to describe the frat culture he hates, Henry pulls Drew outside into the dewy spring night.

"Hey, man," Henry says. "What was that?"

Drew deftly rolls a cigarette. "What do you mean?"

"You know what I mean. Margot."

Drew takes a long, contemplative drag off his cigarette and looks down the block, away from Henry. A group of youths from town, African-Americans, stand in a circle under a streetlamp, and it is a note of dissonance that infects Bannister and other small college towns, the wealthy white kids on the hill, while kids of a different color, for whom college is a distant dream, live down below.

"She's just not you, man," Drew says.

Henry feels the anger rising. "She is me," he says. "She couldn't be more me."

"Look, I love you like a brother; you know that. But girls like her—they're not for guys like us."

"She's different," Henry says.

"You're whipped."

"So what if I am?"

"She drives a convertible Saab," Drew says. "You walk."

"Who gives a fuck what she drives?"

"The universe does, Henry. The universe."

"That's such bullshit."

"Look, you do what you want," Drew says. "I will behave."

And Drew smiles then, and Henry knows he can't stay mad at him. Drew has a way about him, a natural charisma, and they are also feeling out this friendship in the same way they are learning to feel out the world. They are all constantly testing, pushing against things to see which ones give and which ones respond by not moving at all.

Looming in front of Henry that spring is the impending summer. It is something the two of them have not talked about and Henry wants to figure out how they can be together somehow, but summers are tricky for him, as he needs to make money and work, and he knows that she does not have to.

The previous year, he had returned to Providence, living again with his parents, and his father got him a job at a staple factory on the edge of town. It was in a small, windowless aluminum building, eight different machines, with one man on each one. They wore headphones against the noise, but it didn't matter. Henry felt it in his sleep, the constant rat-a-tat of the pounding machines that measured, shaved, and ultimately cut long strips of slender metal.

The guys he worked with were good guys, Portuguese and Italian and Puerto Rican, and at lunch they sat outside in the lee of the building and ate the lunches they had brought with them in lunch boxes and thermoses like schoolchildren, and that is when Henry noticed that many of them were missing fingers. Some had stubs that ended halfway down and others had entire digits gone. It was the price they paid for making $17.50 an hour, good jobs for a nonunion shop. Mostly, though,

Henry enjoyed the quickness of their banter, the back-and-forth, how smart they were. And the greatest compliment, of course, was when they began to give him shit like he was one of them, calling Henry "college boy" and telling him to get out of there before he ended up like them, stuck in this job where the smallest gap in attention could mean a healthy chunk of phalanx was scattering across a cement floor.

And Henry's job was the most dangerous of all. All day long he was expected to stand between these two machines, and when the hot thread of metal came out of one and into the final one, where it was snipped into its ultimate shape, he was expected to use his hands and ensure that it stayed straight and true and didn't fold onto itself. But, he was told, if he held on too long, his fingers could end up in the machine, which might then spit them out unceremoniously onto the floor.

As a result, Henry spent that summer with a focus greater than he had ever had. Sometimes he would find himself staring mindlessly at that endless thin stream of metal and would remind himself to pay attention, but his mind was swimming with poems, with verse and structure and the beauty of the silence that came between words, between stanzas, all that blank space an answer to the constant throbbing noise that required headphones just to block out.

And then at night, Henry wanted nothing to do with the old crowd. Plus, his parents saddened him. In some ways, he thought, you can never truly go home. Oh, he appreciated his mother's cooking, and her chicken soup, in particular, clear and golden, served with bread and schmaltz on the side, always gave him a lift.

But the apartment was smaller than he remembered, his dad was even more withdrawn, his mother doted on him as if he were twelve, and the narrow streets were impossibly humid and hot on summer days, so much so that he longed for nights when they were slick with rain and the ocean breeze reached deep into the neighborhoods and he could sit on the rickety third-floor porch and read with a flashlight and listen to the water cascading all around him.

Henry knew Margot summered on the Vineyard. It was not until he had arrived at Bannister that he had heard *summer* used as a verb. And Martha's Vineyard, while only perhaps forty-five miles away as the crow flies from where he has spent the majority of his life, might as well be on the other side of the planet. Until Margot, he had never met anyone who had ever been there. It is a place for rich people.

And so April turns to May and the summer is almost upon them. One afternoon, one of the English faculty members, a medievalist named O'Neill, stops Henry on the pathway running to the right of the largest quad and asks him about his summer plans. Henry tells him he is not yet sure, and he feels an ache as he says it, knowing that it is hard to imagine a plan that involves Margot, and then the professor asks him if he has any interest in staying here in the Finger Lakes and working at a winery owned by his brother and his brother's wife.

"Hard work," the professor says. "Work in the fields. Sell

wine to tourists. But it comes with housing on the lake. Not much of a place, but good for a poet. If you're interested, I could make an introduction."

Later that afternoon, Henry tells Margot about it, and he hopes she will express disappointment and say, "Oh, I thought you would come to the Vineyard with me," but instead she says that it sounds really cool. And the next day, Henry goes to meet Ted, the professor's brother, a mild-mannered man with a long beard, and his wife, Laura, who is as quiet and serious as his father.

The winery is almost directly opposite Bannister, on the other side of the lake. Henry rides a bike there and it is a day bright with sun and the road to the small winery runs through acres of cornfields and then opens up with ten acres of grapes swooping down to the shimmering blue lake. The winery itself is nestled into a small hillside, so that only the roof is visible, and the front opens onto a sandy driveway. The owners have a house they built, visible across the fields to the south of the winery, and as part of the tour they take him down to show him where he would live if he is offered the job and chooses to accept.

It is a seasonal cabin, though it might be generous to call it that. It was erected originally for a family of migrant workers and has no running water or electricity, only an outhouse in the trees behind it. Inside it has two single beds, a few wooden chairs, and a table. Two small windows look out each side, one back to the vineyard and the other toward the lake. But it is only fifty feet from the shore of the lake and is completely private, and despite the subsistence living, it might be the most beautiful place Henry has ever seen.

"What do I do for water?" Henry asks.

"There is a spring right over there," Ted says. "With a pump. And you can shower up at the house."

Henry laughs. "And no refrigerator?"

"You can eat with us at the house. Meals included. When you want. You might get sick of us. And there is one at the winery. You can keep things in there."

"I guess I always secretly wanted to be a monk," Henry says with a smile.

Henry looks out to the lake then, and with an awareness that will later come to define his poetry, he thinks of how he almost left his fingers behind last summer on the floor of a Providence warehouse, only to live a year later on the shore of a new prodigious one far away from home.

Margot, 1991

The last night together before summer, neither of them wants to sleep. Margot is aware of the imbalance between them, the fact that Henry scraps for a few dollars to buy himself a whiskey and ginger ale a few nights a week at the bar, while thousands flow directly into her bank account every month without her saying so much as a thing about it. But on this night, she says to him that she doesn't want to hear any objections, that this one is on her, and they walk down to the lake on an evening that is summer-hot, to a place Henry has never been, this five-star hotel over the lake that is most famous for being the setting in a scene from the film version of Nabokov's *Lolita*.

They walk into the massive inn with their arms linked, and at the front desk Margot asks for the honeymoon suite, saying it theatrically, and the clerk, a young man barely older than they are, takes her American Express Gold Card and says to both of them, "Congratulations, Mr. and Mrs. Fuller."

"You can call me Henry," Henry says. "Henry Fuller."

And it is the shared joke of the evening, his taking her name, and all night he calls her Mrs. Fuller, and upstairs they check into a room that contains the turret of the castle that is the hotel, and from its windows they look down on the lake below them and can see all the way across to where the land rises again and to where Henry will spend his summer.

It is Henry's eyes that Margot loves the most. Dark eyes that are instantly friendly, eyes that literally twinkle when he is amused, as he is now, looking around at this room and the massive bed with its canopy hanging over it.

"That's not a bed, Mrs. Fuller," Henry says. "It's a goddamn playground."

Margot laughs. "I confess I am very nervous, Mr. Fuller. After all, it is our wedding night."

"I will be patient with you, Mrs. Fuller."

"Not too patient, I hope," Margot says.

Henry picks her up then, and she shrieks when he does. He picks her up and carries her in his arms in an imitation of the groom taking the bride over the threshold, and on the bed he lays her down and then he lies next to her. Margot loves his hands on her, how capable and intuitive they are, and she loves the feel of his weight on her and she loves when she can feel his breath start to become ragged and she knows he is close, that she has done this to him, that they have done this to each other.

Downstairs after, they are seated in the formal dining room at a table that replicates the same view they had upstairs. There is one other couple in here, old enough to be her grandparents, but otherwise it is just the two of them. Henry's eyes are wide and he says to her, "I have a confession."

"What is it?"

He smiles. "I've never been in a restaurant with tablecloths before."

"No," she says. "Really? How is that possible?"

Henry shrugs. "My mother cooked. We never went out. Ever. And if we had, we weren't in places like this."

And Margot loves this about Henry: She has never met anyone like him before. There is no carefully constructed facade to him like all the other boys have, most of them practicing to become their fathers, down to the talk of Republican politics and money and the market and already choosing their drink, scotch often, or the gin and tonics of summer. It is as if he is without guile; born somehow into this moment as white and clean as the tablecloths he is eating on for the first time.

That night they make love in the huge bed and afterward they lie facing each other, their arms around each other, mouths only inches away, their noses almost close enough to touch. Henry's breath is hot on her face, and when they talk, they whisper, but mostly they just look into each other's eyes. She has never felt so close to anyone before, didn't know it was possible to feel so close to someone, and the very idea of it threatens to overwhelm her for a moment, and before she starts to cry, Henry takes her face in his strong hands and holds it.

"I love you," she whispers.

"You have no idea how much I love you," he says.

"I think I do," she says.

"You cannot," he says.

"I don't want to fight," she says, smiling in the dark at him.

"Never," Henry says.

In the morning, Henry helps her load up her Saab until it is full to the brim and the only space that is open is the driver's seat. All around them the school is emptying out for the summer. A steady rain falls, but they don't care. Margot opens her arms and Henry takes her in his. The rain is soaking both of them. She doesn't want him to stop holding her, but after a while Henry pulls back and looks at her. He pushes her wet hair off her forehead. He says, "You should go."

And then they step away from each other. For what seems a long time, Margot stands with her hand on the door of her car, and she knows her lip is quivering, and there is the rain falling, and it is like they have been sucked apart, a vacuum releasing, and now they are on their own.

Driving away down South Main Street toward the highway, Margot stares in the side mirrors—she can't see out the back—until he fades, growing smaller and smaller, and then disappears completely.

Henry, Henry, Henry, she thinks.

Eight hours later, the rain has stopped and the skies have cleared and Margot drives her car onto the ferry at Woods

Hole. She parks and climbs up to the top deck, where people sit on blue benches, watching the ocean. The sun has just gone down, and the moon has already risen in the east, a crescent sliver. This is normally a trip she relishes, that feeling of leaving the mainland, of getting to the island, of knowing summer is in front of her, but tonight she stares out at the rolling chop as the ferry moves across the sound and she feels an emptiness as vast as the water to her starboard side sweep over her.

Margot drives off the ferry at Oak Bluffs and now it is completely dark, and on those familiar roads heading up-island with the windows down, she can smell the ocean breeze, and the uniformly planted trees are lined like sentinels at the roadside.

She passes through a few small villages with little more than a general store, and soon she is into Chilmark and turning off on the sandy road that leads to the house her father built ten years ago by tearing down an farmhouse on the beach and replacing it with a six-thousand-square-foot house. At the time it was controversial, the idea that in this section of the island, where things changed slowly, someone would take down one of those great old weathered-shingled homes and replace it with something four times the size.

But as in many things, Margot's father was in fact ahead of his time, a pioneer, he might tell you, and before long it was happening all over the island and six thousand square feet seemed like an appropriately scaled summer shack in comparison to some of the houses that went up after he built his.

The house is lit like the sun. Light streams from every window. Margot comes into the broad foyer with the chandelier hanging down like an ornament, a nod to her mother, and then through and into the kitchen.

Her mother sees her first. "Look who is here!" she exclaims, and comes to her. Her father is against the granite island, rows of tumbler glasses in front of him filled with ice, a bottle of gin in his hand. He looks up and smiles. They have company, of course.

"Honey," her mother says, and hugs her. Her mother is all perfume and hair, and underneath Margot smells the slightly dank smell of the cigarette she recently sneaked in the composed but wild-crafted landscape between the dunes and the ocean.

Her father gives her a broad smile across the counter. "Come here," he says, not stopping making the gin and tonics.

Margot goes to him and leans into him and her father puts his arm around her. He has on his summer uniform, shorts and a polo shirt.

"How's Danny?" her father says.

"He's great," says Margot, lying. She has no idea how Danny is.

"Well, I hope he comes down this summer. Good kid."

"We'll see," Margot says.

"Help me with these drinks. The Baldwins are here."

Outside on the fieldstone patio, there is a fire in the large stone pit that sits in the middle of it, and on either side of it sit her parents' friends, who rise and each give her a hug. Beyond them in the dark Margot can hear the incessant slap of the ocean.

"Sit down with us," her mother says. "Have a drink."

"Chad will be down on Monday," Mrs. Baldwin says. "I know he'll look forward to seeing you." Chad is their son, who goes to Colby, in Maine. Margot kissed him once in high school. He is handsome in a toothy kind of way. Ever since they were little kids, there has been an effort to put the two of them together.

"I think I'm going to lie down," Margot says. "Long drive."

"Of course, honey," her mother says.

"Good to see you all," Margot says.

"Welcome home," they say in return.

Upstairs, Margot lies on her bed fully clothed in the dark. With the window open, their empty conversations float up to her, just voices on the air, the gin-soaked laughter of a crude joke landing, and in the distance she can hear the surf.

Margot is pleased with the solitude. In a few days, her sister and her fiancé will join them on the island. The summer will kick into gear. There will be sun-drenched days on the beach. Clambakes. Afternoons punctuated by cocktail hours that arrive earlier and earlier.

But tonight she can be deliciously alone in her bed with Henry. She can replay that moment when they said good-bye. She can see his black eyes pleading with her not to go. She can feel his hands on her in the hotel bed from the night before. And this is the part of love no one tells you about: that you can be far apart and if you close your eyes and push your face into the pillow, you can reach across time and space and for a few moments before you fall asleep you can be together for as long as you like.

Henry, 1991

Henry is not afraid of hard work. At the winery, the day starts at dawn, and for the first time in his life he fires a gun. Henry rises with the sun and makes his way to the house, always with some trepidation, for Ted and Laura, the owners, have an Australian cattle dog, which never seems to learn that Henry belongs here. Henry has a fear of dogs that comes from growing up in his Providence neighborhood, where few people actually owned dogs and those who did owned ones meant to deter people from coming into their apartments.

Ted cooks breakfast for the three of them, and it is as if they are a family, Henry thinks, eating eggs at the table, with its view of the blue expanse of lake. Afterward, Henry and Ted go to the winery, where they sit on the rooftop with the acres of grapes below them. Ted teaches Henry how to use a shotgun and the day begins by firing over the grapes at the huge murder of crows that descends every morning to try to eat the grapes. The goal is not to actually kill the birds, but, rather, to make them fly away. And Henry is happy about this strategy, for he doesn't want to kill anything, though on his third day he levels the shotgun and takes one of the huge black birds right out of the sky. Watching it flutter down takes his breath away, and when they discover it a few minutes later, dead between the rows, Henry feels sick about it and Ted laughs at him.

"It's okay to hit a few, Henry," Ted says. "They're terrible thieves."

There are hot mornings when they spend hours on their knees amid the ten acres of grapes, pruning by hand each individual plant. Henry likes the labor and he has the focus of a poet, and Ted teaches him about the grapes, the different varieties; the pinot noir and the chardonnay, the sauvignon blanc and the Riesling, the black-as-night merlot and the cabernet. For lunch, Laura brings them sandwiches and they eat cross-legged in the fields and open a bottle of wine, and Henry loves this, the sun hot on his face, drinking wine from the bottle and feeling the sweat of the morning's labor.

The afternoons and rainy days are spent inside the cool, dark winery, and Ted teaches him how they fill the bottles from the wooden casks—in the case of the red wine—and from the stainless-steel tanks—in the case of the whites. They bottle by hand, they cork them by hand, and then they apply the labels one at a time. It is simple and beautiful work, and Henry thinks Ted and Laura might be the happiest people he has ever met. They have this spit of land on the lake and they have each other. They roll out of bed and into their jobs. At night, they cook beautiful meals and always there is wine. They welcome Henry into their home; it is the old-fashioned life of a farmhand and he loves it.

At night in his small cabin, Henry reads by the light from the oil lamp, and often he is bone-tired and the morning is unforgiving, but in the dimly lit quiet he forces himself to work, writing at the desk with a bottle of wine. It is a discipline, he reminds himself, like learning to play shortstop, and he practices with the same attention to his poetry as he once did with his glove, when he would take grounder after grounder until it was second nature, until he could read the hop before the ball even came off the grass.

And amid it all in that first week is Margot. It is as if Henry has built a new cabin in his mind where she lives, a finished poem she is, a place he can summon whenever he chooses and sometimes when he does not. When he is working in the fields, images of her come to him: those eyes, her laugh, her strong legs, how she tilts her head and closes her eyes softly when he reads to her.

There is something else, too: a nagging sense of self-doubt. All new loves are like a dream, but sometimes he wonders if Margot is a mirage, and Henry reassures himself by remembering the small particulars of their parting, how she clearly didn't want to go, the magic of that last night, when they held each other until the sun rose above the lake.

But she also didn't invite him to the island, and while she

left him the phone number for her house, she knows he doesn't have a phone other than at Ted and Laura's, and it is in their kitchen and they are always there, it seems, and in the first days at the winery he is not yet comfortable enough to ask them if he can use it.

After dinner on his third night there, Henry walks down to the water from his cabin. The night is humid and on his arms is a shine from the heat. At the water's edge he looks out, and far across he can see the tops of some of the buildings of Bannister, the rise of the clock tower on Bishop Hall interrupting the sky above the trees.

Henry strips off his clothes and leaves them in a pile at the lake's edge. Then he wades into the cool water until it's above his knees and then he dives, going under and then coming back up, doing the crawl until he is far out and can float on his back. From out here he can look both ways, to two different worlds, close but far apart: the college and the winery. One contains Margot. The other does not.

That night at his writing desk, Henry counts the days till school starts again. There are fifty-three from today. He takes a clean piece of paper and on the top of it he writes in blocky numbers and letters *53 things I miss about you.*

Number 53, he writes. *That you want to watch me write as if that is something that can be watched.*

And so Henry makes his list. It is a test of sorts, for it seems like it should be hard to come up with that many, but they roll off his pen with ease. He talks about her laughter, what a beautiful peal it is, echoing in his head; he talks about how she loves to talk after sex, how it makes her manic; he says he loves that her eyes are the color of a foreign sea; he describes the place where her hip meets her leg, the subtle rise and curve of her. He says he loves hearing her say his name, how she says it differently depending on the circumstances, like how Eskimos have so many words for snow, each iteration of "Henry" meaning something slightly different. He loves her love of ice cream and her unabashed appetite in general, that she will dive into a burger with a relish he is used to associating with baseball teammates. He says he saw tears in her eyes only once, when they were parting, but that he longs to see her cry, even though he doesn't want to feel what she cries for.

Number 1, he writes. *You, just you, all of you, my Margot.*

In the end, Henry fills three pages of paper. He thinks about rereading them but then reminds himself one of the lessons he learned in creative writing: Don't self-edit too quickly. This is not a poem, he tells himself. You do not need to sculpt it.

He folds the paper up and puts it into an envelope and addresses it to Margot, using the address she gave him for the house on the Vineyard. And in the morning, he mails it from Ted and Laura's house.

Margot, 1991

Margot comes in from the beach, and as she is on her way upstairs to change out of her suit, the stack of mail on the front table catches her eye. She moves toward it and she sees the letter and the return address and then she bounds up the stairs and into the bathroom, where she locks the door behind her.

Her fingers are shaking as she peels the seal away and takes out the folded pieces of paper. She opens them and begins to read and a smile comes across her face. She sinks to the floor, with her back against the tiled wall, and reads the three pages rapidly and then reads them again and again.

In the days that follow, Margot takes the pages with her everywhere. She considers making a list of her own, but she is not a writer like Henry is: She wouldn't even know where to begin. Oh, there are things she could say, about his lack of pretension, how he is different from any boy she has ever known. But she could never capture the particularity of him in the way he has captured the particularity of her, and later, when this all sinks in, she will come to realize that this might be the greatest gift another person can give you. The very idea that they pay enough attention to notice what makes you singular, and Margot has no idea how she can possibly repay him.

But she does. She can commit an act of defiance, and not even a big one, for her entire life she has moved in small orbits, concentric circles of the same people, the same places, and this is what it means to be wealthy in America: You see small slices of life, the same cities, the same islands, the same people. Vast tracts of the country are off-limits to you, and while upstate New York is a fine place to go to college, there is no discernible reason to be there in the summer. Except that for Margot, now there is.

One morning she comes downstairs to find her father in the foyer with his suitcase packed, looking at his watch and then out the window to the driveway.

"Where are you going?" Margot asks.

"Singapore for a few days, if the car ever gets here," he says. "No rest for the wicked," he adds, and smiles.

That night, Margot invites her mother for a walk. They head out through the dunes and onto the open beach. It is a beautiful evening and the number of people on the private beach is sparse—a few runners moving along the water, people walking dogs. There is not much wind and the surf is light, but it is open ocean and it still falls heavily against the hard sand, and as Margot wants to be as close to the water as she can, she and her mother have to raise their voices to be heard.

"There's a boy," Margot says.

"Your father told me. He thinks highly of him."

"It's not Danny."

"Oh?"

"No, there is another one. His name is Henry."

Her mother looks at her oddly, and for a moment they stop. Margot glances past her mother to the long length of beach, to how the water laps and recedes, laps and recedes.

"I don't understand," her mother says.

"Daddy wouldn't like him," Margot says.

"Why, is he black?"

"Mom, no. And that is so racist. It shouldn't matter."

"Well, I don't see what the problem is, then. Is it serious?"

"I love him," Margot says.

"Where is he?"

"He's back at school. Working for the summer."

Margot's mother looks alarmed. "Back at school? Is he a professor, Margot, is that why? He's older?"

"No, no. He's a student."

Her mother looks relieved. "I can't imagine what it is with this boy that your father would be upset about. He's quite reasonable, Margot, you know."

"You know how Daddy can be," says Margot.

"Your father always wants the best for you. That is true. And so do I."

Margot looks away to the ocean then, and far away on the

horizon she sees the outline of a container ship. For some reason, she wonders how the big ships from a distance always look like they are standing still, when of course they must be moving. Out there on the curvature of the earth, a large, still form, and she suddenly wishes she had decided against this conversation.

As if sensing this, her mother says, "What is he like, this boy?"

Margot looks back at her mother. "He's sweet. Kind. He writes poetry. He used to be a baseball player."

Her mother nods, as if weighing this sparse information. "Where is he from?"

"Providence."

"Rhode Island?"

Margot sighs. "Yes."

"Why don't you invite him to visit? He can stay in the guest room," her mother says.

"He can't," Margot says back. "He has to work."

Her mother considers this. "Well, nothing wrong with work, I suppose."

"I need a favor," Margot says. "I need to go see him. But I don't want Dad to know."

"I'm not in the business of hiding things from your father."

"I need this. I just need to know. Do you remember that feeling? Of first being with someone? And how hard it is to be apart?"

Her mother looks back toward the dunes, which from this

angle obscure where the house is, and then back to Margot. She smiles slightly. "Of course," she says.

"Then help me," Margot says.

Her mother is silent for a moment and they start walking again. "You have one week," her mother says.

Margot smiles broadly. She moves to her right and hugs her smaller mother from behind, her head on her mother's shoulder like a lover. "What about Daddy?"

"I will take care of that," her mother says. She smiles back at Margot. "We haven't lasted this long without my knowing how to handle him. Now go."

An hour later, Margot is on the ferry. The night is clear and the ocean stars bend in a great arc away from her. Normally when she is leaving the island, she looks back with sadness as that hump of land surrounded by sea gets smaller and smaller in the wake of the boat. The place she most identifies with as home. Tonight, though, she stands on the other side, staring at the horn of mainland in front of her. She faces Henry, part of a continent away.

Henry, 2012

One weekend a month, Henry has Jess. Sometimes he drives up and picks her up in Tarrytown and brings her back, and other times Ruth drives her into the city. In the summer, he will often pick her up on his way to Vermont. Henry both looks forward to the weekends and fears them. Henry tries to be kind to Ruth in those brief moments when they see each other, though there is always this exasperated tension between them, more her than him, Henry thinks, which strikes him as fundamentally unfair, for when a marriage unravels, there is plenty of blame to go around, and his crimes are more crimes of omission.

Ruth left him, after all, not the other way around. She was the one who had the affair—with a college administrator, of all things, an accountant type with a name, Steve Johnson, as bland as the work he did. And while Henry was furious when she first told him, in time he came to realize that the affair was as much his decision as it was hers. Henry had turned his back on Ruth a long time ago. For he had married the wrong woman and he knew it even before that rainy day in late May when they went down to city hall with a few friends and made it official.

Henry was not sure he loved Ruth and he wasn't sure Ruth loved him. Later, he would remember advice he had gotten from Jon, his college teacher, who told him never to marry another writer.

"There is too much jealousy involved," Jon said. "What if she is more successful than you are? What if you are? It never works. Trust me."

And perhaps this was part of it, for Henry won the Yale Younger Poets prize, and later he found out that Ruth had been in contention for it as well. She congratulated him in all the proper and appropriate public ways, but underneath it all Henry sensed that she believed she was the more talented of the two of them, that part of his winning was sexism and that voice of his, how personal it was, the way he summoned his youth and poverty and the raw specificity of his own experiences. He didn't go universal the way Ruth did, at least not as easily, and Henry knew she resented him for it at the same time that she did her best to rise above it and celebrate it.

But then she was pregnant and here they were, both young faculty members with the same circle of friends, and everything became inevitable in a way that both of them seemed to understand but didn't seem at liberty to do anything about, as if you somehow gave up free will in your thirties. They moved into marriage and parenthood with smiles on their faces, both good people, they told themselves, who would make it all work. And for a time, it did.

They both wrote. They tended to the baby as if she were a hearth. Jess had his black eyes and Ruth's crazy mess of hair and she was a perfect mash-up of the two of them. And soon she was no longer a baby, but a pretty girl. They had stable careers—as stable as poets in academia can be. They were both publishing.

But they were also drifting apart, the way people do. Henry was too much in his head, Ruth said.

"You're never present," she told him once.

"I don't know what you mean," he said.

"Present with me. You live in your head."

"Don't you?"

"No, Henry, I don't. I don't have that luxury."

And in hindsight, Henry probably should have known his marriage was over then, that the two of them were playing out the string, going through the motions that constitute a shared life.

But instead he ignored all the signs, and even as he became less and less emotionally available to Ruth, he continued to move forward with plans, as if the future in front of them was bright. They left the city for the leafy quiet of Tarrytown. Jess learned to ride a bike. She could run outside around the neighborhood on her own with other kids. Henry and Ruth had dinner together with Jess, but otherwise they were becoming more and more separate people. In private, and late at night when he couldn't sleep, Henry would spend hours on his computer, trying to find Margot. How does someone, in this time, not leave any footprints? he wondered.

And it was as if he had two lives, the one he dwelled in every day, and the one he could access only in the dark of the night, when he and those in his neighborhood lay sleeping and he could reach deep into the pocket of memory and there was Margot.

Sometimes he picked up his collection, *Margaret,* the one that had won him the Yale prize, and read through it. It was more an act of bearing witness than anything else, this book, and on those pages he found turns of phrase, like your "sea-wet eyes" and "those half-formed moments before dawn when I didn't want the world to wake because it meant I had to share you."

At critical moments in his life—the day, for instance, that Ruth told Henry about the affair with Steve Johnson, laying it on him casually one morning while they both sat in the breakfast nook having coffee, as if it were just another piece of information he needed to know, as banal as an upcoming dentist appointment—Henry would go find that collection of his, fall into its pages, and feel the cruelty of life engulf him like fog.

Part of the cruelty was not just the mistakes he had made, the things he had let get away from him—though that was part of it—but also the knowledge when reading his own book that he would never write anything more important.

Henry would never again write anything as strong. Winning the Yale prize was supposed to mean a long and illustrious career. But Henry knew that Margot had given him the book that would define who he was the rest of his life. His muse had become just someone he used to know.

Margot, 2012

In the morning, she leaves the hotel in a soft rain; she has a black umbrella from the hotel and the rain is warm and nice. Margot stops at a small kosher bagel place on Amsterdam and she thinks she wants a bagel, but the Hasid behind the counter is rude and angry at everyone, and she suddenly decides she isn't hungry. She does get coffee in a to-go cup and then she is back out into the rain.

It is early. The night before, Margot ordered room service and ate on her bed and watched a bad movie. She tried to focus on the movie because now, back in the relative quiet of the hotel room, she was aware that she was acting like a madwoman, putting her whole life at risk, and for what?

She drank half a bottle of decent red wine and fell asleep with the television on, and she did not dream. She woke with no sense of what time it was, and with the big chandelier above her head coming into focus, it took her a moment to remember where she was. She looked at the clock and she bolted out of bed and into the shower. She couldn't help herself. Was Henry a morning person? Did he stay up late? She couldn't remember. Of course, that was so long ago.

Like the afternoon before, Margot takes a left onto his street, and this morning she is happy for the rain and the umbrella, which feels like a disguise. She moves down the street on the opposite side of his building, and when she is directly across from it, she finds a spot under a tree and slightly to the left of the front door of the nondescript place across, as if she is a woman on her way to work, just casually waiting for her car to show up, albeit wearing a baseball hat.

Margot waits. In the buildings around her, men and women march out with their bags and their work clothes and move briskly past her. No one pays her any attention at all. Every time the door to Henry's building opens, she holds her breath and has this urge to duck into shadows that don't exist at this time of day and in this rain.

A half hour goes by. To move her legs, she walks at one point to the end of the block and then returns to her station again. She is nervous that perhaps she missed him, and then she chides herself for this silliness. For all she knows, he doesn't have a class until the afternoon. She could be standing here all day.

Yet she cannot move. Has she lost her mind? Has she somehow become again the girl she once was, the one who did things impulsively, even if they could ruin everything?

After about an hour, though, Margot's patience is rewarded, though she doesn't know it at first. A late-model Volvo wagon comes slowly down the street from the east. It is dark red and loud, and clearly needs a new exhaust pipe. It stops in front of Henry's building.

The woman driving has a thick head of curly hair and she gets out of the car with the engine still running and walks around to the other side. Margot can see a child in the back, and the woman opens the back door and for a moment the child is shielded from Margot's view, but then Margot sees the door to Henry's building open and here is Henry himself, fifty yards away from her, in jeans and a button-down shirt. The child runs to him, and Margot can see now it is a little girl. She leaps up into Henry's arms and he picks her up in one smooth motion. Margot takes a step back at first, and then removes her phone and pretends to be on it. She looks away, then glances back to the scene across the street.

"Sunday at noon," Margot hears Henry say to the woman, who has not moved closer to Henry than when she opened the door to the car. Henry's voice goes right through Margot, rich and resonant, though she can still hear the trace of a nasally accent, which she is glad he has not lost.

The woman blows a kiss to the little girl, who Margot can see is adorable, as all children that age are. She has her mother's curls and they tumble down on either side of her face. Black buttons for eyes. Henry puts the girl down and goes to the door of the building and opens it, though he doesn't go in, just reaches in and comes out with an umbrella. The Volvo drives slowly away. Henry opens the umbrella and takes the girl's hand in his own. The two of them begin to walk away from Margot toward Amsterdam.

It is a small moment she has just witnessed, more of a ritual than anything, one that plays out across the country on weekends and one that tells her in an instant a lot about Henry's life. He is divorced and this is his daughter. She lives with her mother somewhere else.

While there is nothing intimate in any of this that has been revealed, Margot, standing in the rain, watching them walk away from her, nevertheless feels a tinge of shame for having watched it. But, after all, it is public space, isn't it? It's not like she has sneaked into his apartment under the cover of darkness, right?

Margot looks up the street and sees that the two of them are halfway up the block. She should leave now for Darien and go back to her life before she puts everything in jeopardy. But she has come this far. She begins to walk after them.

On busy Amsterdam, Margot struggles to keep up with the two of them, losing them briefly in the crowd of people with umbrellas making its way down the avenue. But then she spies them just in time before they take a left and head toward Columbus. When she turns onto quiet Eighty-first Street, she once again shares the side street with them, though they are almost at the end of the block, and oblivious to her, a father and daughter holding hands and moving toward, she imagines, the park.

But then on Columbus, Margot watches as they cross the street, heading to Central Park West, and then there is the great facade of the American Museum of Natural History. She has the memory of taking her own children here, how it was once the most magical place on earth for the two of them, the awe they had looking at the *Barosaurus* in the lobby, the taxidermy animals that appeared as if they might at any moment leave their perches and scoop small children into their huge mouths. This memory pangs her a little bit—what a thief time is—but she knows without a doubt this is where Henry is going.

Margot gives them a ten-minute head start and then she enters the building as well. She has this immediate fear that the security people will figure her out and detain her, for she has to be only the middle-aged woman in the place without at least one child at her side. But this is, of course, silly. Thousands of people pass through these doors every day.

And so Margot follows Henry and his daughter through the museum. She tries to keep her distance, staying half an exhibit away, though at one point she loses the two of them in the Hall of Gems. Margot is standing looking at a topaz display when she hears Henry's voice, and it moves through her like electricity.

"Look at this, Jess," he says, and that is how Margot learns his daughter's name.

The two of them are right behind her. If she was to turn around, she would be face-to-face with them. Her heart is in her throat, and for a moment she imagines doing just this, turning around, his daughter a buffer between the two of them, a governor ensuring the encounter is brief and casual. It will be nothing more than old friends saying hello.

But Margot slides to her left, as if moving to the next display, and she feels them displace her, moving toward the topaz, and now she just keeps moving, out of the room and the space they just shared.

Outside, the rain has stopped, but the air smells of it, warm and wet. Margot stands for a moment outside the giant stone building. Her heart feels like it might spring out of her body. She is as alive as an animal, wanting to run into the park like a deer and vanish into the trees.

Henry, 1991

The night is unseemly hot and Henry sleeps with the cabin door open. Because of the heat, he sleeps unevenly, and when he does sleep, the dreams come in waves—there is Margot underneath him and he is moving above her and then suddenly she is there but not there, her face as blank as a sheet of paper. She has no eyes and no nose and no mouth. He wakes at one point in a sweat and beyond the open door the land leading down to the lake is blue with moonlight.

He drifts in and out of sleep, and when the first yellow of dawn comes, he wakes with a start, as if from a sound, and now looking out, he sees the land is full of heavy mist, as it often is this close to the lake. Henry knows that if he was to walk outside, his world would shrink to the several feet in front of him. And then, thinking this and looking out, Henry suddenly sees someone, an outline in the low-hanging fog that begins to take shape, and he feels all his muscles tense intuitively, and a moment later it is as if he still dreaming, for there is Margot, leaning against the doorframe, looking toward where he lies on the bed.

"Knock, knock," she says.

"Holy shit, you scared me," Henry says.

"Get over here," Margot says.

Henry climbs out of bed and goes to her. Margot steps inside the doorway and in the dark he takes her into his arms and she says, "I love the smell of you."

"Sweaty," he whispers, and she laughs.

Henry pulls her to him tight and buries his face in her hair, and then he pulls back and holds her face in his hands and they kiss. For a long while they are silent, holding each other, and it is a game of chicken they are playing, neither of them wanting to pull away, and Henry finally breaks the silence by saying, "I can't believe it's you. That you're here."

"I needed you," Margot says.

After a time they go to the bed, and when they make love, it is with a deep urgency and Henry reminds himself to be slow, but this morning he cannot and afterwards, Margot is crying and he thinks he has done something wrong, but she whispers that she is just so happy to be with him and he knows what she means, that love like this is far closer to insanity than it is to reality, the world around them spinning uncontrollably, and their ability to be together is the only thing holding them on the planet. We *are* gravity, he thinks as he uses his thumb to wipe the tears away from her eyes.

Margot, 1991

The days are midsummer-long, and after a few of them in a row, they begin to take on a routine. Henry wakes with the sun to work in the vineyard and leaves her lying in bed in the small cabin. It feels gloriously unfair to watch him go out the door while she gets to curl back into the pillows and sleep. After work, they swim in the lake, stripping off their clothes at the shore and skinny-dipping, and their second night there they have dinner at Ted and Laura's house, and it is surprising to Margot to see how they interact with Henry, how comfortable he is there, opening the fridge like it's his own, and then how they all pitch in to help cook.

Ted roasts a chicken, and Margot marvels at the simplicity of people preparing food, since in her life she has never cooked a thing. Her parents always had a chef or they ate out. She loves watching how he rubs the bird down with olive oil and garlic and rosemary, how it seems so easy and natural. While the bird cooks, Laura announces that they are going to make baklava.

"That means you, Margot," she says.

"Me? No. I have no idea."

"Don't worry, it's easy."

And so in that rustic kitchen with the wide-pane windows that peer out toward the wide blue lake, the four of them lay out rolls of pastry. Margot is in charge of walking back and forth with a small saucepan full of melted butter and a pastry brush and painting, in long strokes, the butter onto the pastry.

Before dinner, the four of them step outside, and while the dog runs off barking into the vines, they stand on the porch and smoke a joint that Ted has rolled.

Now this is something, Margot thinks, smoking pot with older people, and as the joint goes around, Ted unwinds a story about some crazy friend they knew from high school, how he drove his car into the lake after leaving their house one night. The story is meant to be funny and everyone laughs hard, though for Margot her laughter isn't genuine, for the pot is making her reflective and she hears only bits and pieces. Looking out to the lake and into the fat evening sun still high above the hills, she feels like nothing has ever been more beautiful, and watching the way Ted and Laura feed off each other, the quiet Laura and the gregarious Ted with the smile in his eye as he unfurls a tale he has undoubtedly told dozens of times, she begins to imagine a future with Henry, something beyond just this moment they are living in.

Margot is ravenous. She is ravenous for the chicken, for

the pinot noir they drink with it, for the roasted potatoes, and for the endive salad with pears. She is ravenous for the simple urgency of this moment in time, of watching Ted and Laura make each other laugh, and she can't help but think of her own parents, who surround themselves constantly with other people. As a result, she came to think that this is what marriage is, the need never to be alone with each other so as not to face the fact that you don't really have anything to say to each other.

Most of all, she is ravenous for Henry, for his dark eyes and his smile, the way he looks over at her when Ted makes another joke, some of them lame, but it doesn't matter. It doesn't matter at all, for Henry is right here, not overly solicitous, but instead bringing her in, saying with his eyes, Be with me, just be with me. Please.

In the dark, they walk back through a row of vines to the cabin. The path is narrow and they are wine-drunk and above them the moon is high in the sky and bright enough that the sea of stars is opaque as if behind a veil.

Margot leans into Henry as they walk, more of a stumble really, and at one point, walking between the rows of grapes, he trips on a root or something and then they are both going down, laughing as they fall. He falls on her, she falls on him, and Margot rolls on top of him. Her hair hangs down and obscures her face. Henry is laughing. She pins him now with her knees on his arms.

"Oh, is that how we're doing it?" he says.

"Yes, yes," Margot says, and the lust roiling inside her is so intense that it almost scares her, and for a moment as she stands to wriggle out of her jeans, it is as if she has left her own body, the line between control and madness blurry, and when she gets back on top of Henry, the herbaceous smell of the vines all around them, she wants to bite him hard.

Later, when Henry snores next to her on his back on the small bed, Margot listens to him, the rise and fall of his breath, and she looks out the doorway to the moonlit stretch of field that leads down to the lake. She cannot sleep. She lies on her back. The bed is small and Henry at one point slings a heavy arm over her as he moves to his side.

His body against her is warm. She presses back into him, just to feel the unconscious response, his moving back into her instinctively. Bodies come together and then fall apart. There is something simple and yet profound about this. She remembers the first tentative steps of becoming a woman. Boys she kissed, boys she let touch her, boys she touched, losing her virginity on a beach under the stars and liking the warmth of the moment but left afterward wondering if this was it. She remembers thinking about sex as something she enjoyed having done, rather than something she enjoyed doing. There was the rite of passage to it all, and when she was younger, she just wanted to be a girl who had done things. There was also, of course, the growing sense of power that she had. Those moments when she took a boy into her hand and sometimes her mouth and heard the gasp from him, this separate entity that she could own somehow, a living, sentient thing, and it was easy, boys were easy, if you knew what to do.

But then Henry, and suddenly it is as if a window on an entirely new world has been opened to her, and she has never told anyone about the feelings she has, what he does to her, not even Cricket, for she doesn't believe she would understand. She considers all the other couples she knows, and it is as if they are separate even when they are together. An elaborate theater put on for everyone else, and perhaps just to make it appear as if you are capable of feeling something. With Henry, half the time she doesn't where she ends and he begins anymore.

The light outside the cabin doors is already starting to change when Margot finally drifts off to sleep. The land outside is gradually lightening. She dreams of oceans, the great blue-gray Atlantic, and then fragments she cannot piece together: looking down at Henry at the bottom of the staircase; her mother in a bed, yelling at her; riding in the back of a car moving swiftly through a thick woods. And then there is a voice, her father's, and Margot comes to with a start.

"Get up, get dressed," he says.

Her sleep-wet mind takes a moment to understand what she is seeing in front of her. The sun is up. Her father is standing over their bed. Henry is snoring away, unaware that anything is happening at all.

Henry, 2012

Sometimes Henry looks at Jess and the love he has for her threatens to overwhelm him, more so as she has grown, for when she was a baby, he felt this distance from her that he never told anyone about, and he thought at the time that maybe there was a coldness to his heart that he didn't want to admit.

It is different for women, of course, for he remembers his wife holding Jess when she was tiny and how it changed her: Her very looks seemed to soften, and as long as Jess wasn't crying or sick, Ruth became beatific around their daughter, aglow with the power of making something that could only, by definition, be perfect.

Henry, on the other hand, felt on the outside of it all, staring into a book with a story in which he was just a fringe character. He was supposed to be empathetic and good and yet it was as if none of this had anything to do with him.

But then Jess grew and his worry that this distance he felt from her when she was a baby fell away. Soon, as daughters do, she became his sun and his moon and his stars, and then she was walking, and the fear he had of wanting to protect her from all the dark corners of life kept Henry up at night.

This was one of the many differences between him and Ruth. For while Ruth was a poet, too, she did not have a poet's temperament. He would never have told her this, but her strength as a writer was a workmanlike devotion to the craft, her willingness to pore over language like a scientist. But she lacked imagination. And the same was true, Henry thought in those early years, when it came to Jess, her ability to let her live and grow and get hurt, as if she was someone else's child, not one they had made together, of which there was only one.

Of course this was absurd, and Henry knew it, and oftentimes he admired Ruth for how she parented, how easily it all came to her, the practicality with which she went about it. Later, when his marriage was failing, he sometimes wondered if it wasn't really about the affair and more about his desire to run from death, from the responsibility of his daughter, and his poetic sense that catastrophe just had to lie around every corner for the ones he loved. For this is the great paradox of life, isn't it? The more you love someone, the more that person will eventually break your heart?

Now, walking through the Great Hall of the American Museum of Natural History for the second time that day, Henry looks down at Jess. Her curly hair falls on either side of her pink face. She is beautiful and without scars literal or metaphorical, which is how it should be at this age. She looks up at him, and for a moment he sees the adult she will be someday, more her mother than him, and as if sensing something in his expression, she takes his hand in her own.

Jess looks up at him. And not for the first time he thinks that while he may have married the wrong woman, they certainly had the right child. And sometimes that should be enough, shouldn't it? Maybe this is why he and Ruth married, so Jess would be in the world. Despite all his regrets, Henry cannot imagine this being undone.

Outside, the rain has stopped, but the day is still gray and all around them are the signs of the rain, the puddles and the mist coming off them. Henry looks down at Jess.

"Cheeseburgers and milk shakes?" he says.

His daughter sticks her tongue out and nods her head rapidly like a puppy.

At the Shake Shack, they order cheeseburgers and fries and a vanilla milk shake for her, a pint of beer for him. They stand for a bit, waiting for their food and for a table to open up, and soon one does and they sit down alongside the bubble window on Columbus Avenue. They sit across from each other, and Henry, so used to eating alone, is itching to look at his phone, though he knows there is no real news there, probably nothing more than departmental e-mails that are as important as pennies.

It is just that he is used to eating alone now and to using the phone as a prop, or a book, which he doesn't have with him. He has to remind himself to be present, and he starts by asking Jess questions about school, which she answers with one word between bites. "Good," she says, and "Cool," she says, until he realizes he is practically asking her yes or no questions and this is no way to draw a child out.

At one point, Henry finds himself gazing out at the street, at the people walking by, the streams of children leaving the museum, while he and his daughter sit in silence like an old married couple.

Suddenly he catches his breath. Amid the hustle and bustle, a lone figure stands across the avenue, looking directly at him. A woman in a baseball hat, not moving at all, her stillness causing her to stand out, a port in the storm.

Margot. It can't be. Henry looks back over at Jess, who's cramming french fries into her mouth, and then he looks back out the window, half expecting her to have vanished, a mirage. But she has actually taken a step forward, and for a moment a bus going by shields her from view, and when the bus passes, Henry looks at her and she smiles weakly back at him.

There is no mistaking her now.

Henry has no idea what to do. His heartbeat is in his neck. He is not alone. He is of half a mind just to punch his way through the window, emerge on the street, crouching, with broken glass spilling around him like something out of a movie, and then rush into traffic. Of course, he cannot do any of those things. He looks over at Jess and then out the window again. She has not moved. Is she waiting for him?

Henry waves and she slowly raises her hand before letting it fall back to her side.

Henry looks at Jess's plate. She has eaten half her burger, which is good for her, and is putting the last of the fries in her mouth.

"All done, honey?" he says.

She nods.

More urgently than he means to, he says, "Okay, let's get out of here."

"I need to pee," Jess says.

"What?" Henry says, aware as soon as he says it that he is acting frantic, and his daughter is just staring at him, confused.

"I have to pee," she says.

"Of course, of course," Henry says. He stands, and so does Jess. Henry turns toward the window. Margot continues to stand there, and he holds up one finger to her, as if to say, Give me a minute, please. Give me a minute.

"This way," Henry says to Jess. "Let's go."

He leads her down the narrow corridor to the bathrooms. At the door of the ladies' room, he tells her to be quick, which he realizes is a totally screwed-up thing to say, and he can see that his tension has Jess's attention, but she just shrugs and goes into the ladies' room, which is crowded. Usually this moment frightens him, that she is old enough that he can leave her in a room full of strangers to drop her pants where he cannot see her. But today Henry just wants her to hurry.

Five minutes later, Jess emerges, and Henry breathes a sigh of relief, which he knows is silly, as if somehow the bathroom would swallow her up, or one of the women in there would somehow decide to sneak by him with Jess smuggled into her coat.

"There you are," Henry says, and he takes her hand. They move through the restaurant and then out the door and onto the street. He panics briefly, as he doesn't instantly see Margot where she stood some ten minutes before. But then he looks straight ahead, across the crosswalk, and she stands there waiting for them.

The light changes and they move across the street.

"Where are we going, Daddy?" Jess asks.

"Just over here. I see someone I know."

And then they are in front of each other, the years peeling away, a moment he has imagined for twenty years now but never really thought would take place. His daughter is on his hand like a balloon he has forgotten he is carrying. They do not hug. They do not embrace. He doesn't shake her hand or anything more formal. They just stand in front of each other there on Columbus Avenue on a summer day when the rain has stopped but the sun has yet to emerge. Margot is shaking. The earth beneath him is shifting. For what seems like an eternity, they just look at each other. Jess is tugging at Henry's hand and he knows he needs to say something, or that Margot needs to say something, but all he can do is look at her eyes, those sea blue eyes, and if anything, to him she is more beautiful than he remembered, for it is only with age that the true character of a woman shows. Someone must break the silence.

"I can't believe it's you," Henry says.

Margot's face looks like it might crack. He can see her fighting it, but despite her efforts, her eyes have begun to well up. Margot looks into his eyes and then she looks down at Jess. In an attempt at normalcy, she says, "This must be your daughter."

"I'm sorry," Henry says. "Yes, this is Jess."

Margot, experienced at this, goes down then and gets on Jess's level. "Let me guess. I think you're ten."

Jess smiles. "Nine. You were close."

"Well, you are adorable. I'm Margot." And she holds her hand out then for his daughter, and his daughter takes it.

And around them the city continues, blind and unaware. Cabs and buses stream by. Horns honk in open defiance of the signs that line the avenue. Around them, everyone is in a hurry, rushing to get somewhere. If poetry is the search for significance, than the stubbornness of love must be its fullest expression.

Margot, 2012

She is still standing, right? Around her is the banal normalcy of the passive city. Margot watches Henry and his daughter walk toward the park as if nothing just happened, the two of them holding hands, a slight skip in his daughter's step, the only hint of anything having happened to Henry is perhaps a little weight to his walk, a slight listing to the right, though that could be age, or just her desire that Henry be suddenly altered by her appearance on a sidewalk across from him.

Margot watches them until they round the corner on Central Park West and disappear. In her hand she holds his business card, such a funny small thing, words and numbers but a tie to Henry that she has not had before, his cell phone number scrawled on it in pen, his hands visibly shaking as he wrote it.

As if on cue, the rain begins again, a soft rain, and Margot is suddenly terribly tired and hungry and she wants now to be back at the hotel, to curl up in her bed after managing to eat something and replay what has just happened in the quiet, anonymous space that only a hotel room can afford.

Margot begins to walk. Back at the hotel, she comes into the small lobby and then to the elevator and up to her room. Now she is more tired than hungry, but she knows she needs to eat, so she orders room service, a burger, which she will only pick at, and a bottle of wine, which she will drink until maybe she can sleep.

When she finally lies down on the bed, having eaten three bites of the expensive burger and a handful of fries, pushing her face into the pillow, Margot sees Henry as he was earlier, standing in front of her, the dutiful father with a lovely child connected to his fingers. She sees the way he looked at her, the pregnancy of his eyes, wanting to burst with all that had been stolen from him.

And here is the paradox of time: Looking at him, Margot felt like Henry knows her better than anyone ever has. And yet he learned just in that moment that she had two children, that she was married, that she lived in Darien. And while she knows that gives a certain portrait, one that saddens her, the cliché of the wealthy housewife in her big house, within that life she has lived since she last saw him are the multitudes of details that one cannot possibly explain in a streetside meeting, and that collectively make her who she is. Could he actually know her? Or does he know only the girl frozen in time from a lifetime ago?

Oh, what a folly this is! What is she doing, exactly? Following an old boyfriend around the city, manufacturing a run-in? One that could undo all she has managed to build in the last twenty years?

Margot pushes her face farther into the pillow. Sometimes she wishes you could just turn life off like a switch, and everything would go dark. She starts to cry. She cries for Henry because she could see the sadness in his face, but mostly she cries for herself, for the woman she has become, how entrenched she is in a life she suddenly isn't sure she wants anymore. She falls asleep.

The ringing of her phone wakes her up.

Margot is disoriented: She has no idea whether it is day or night, or even where she is. She remembers, of course, that she is in the hotel room, though the heavy curtains are drawn, blocking out either the light or the night. She rolls over and sees that it is her husband calling.

Margot answers it with a hello.

"Where are you?"

"What do you mean?"

"Well," Chad says. "I'm home and you are not here."

Margot tries to wipe the fog out of her mind. How long has she been here? She is certain Chad wasn't due home until tomorrow.

"Where are you?" Chad asks for the second time, not stern yet, just trying to figure it out.

"In the city," she says, getting up now while she talks, looking around the room frantically, as if he might come rushing through that door.

"Shopping?"

"A little," Margot says. "Met Cricket for a drink."

"You drove," says Chad.

Did she? Of course she did. It seems forever ago that the hotel valeted her car. "Yes, I was running late for the train."

"Okay, well, are you heading back? There's nothing to eat here. I was thinking of calling in for some Thai."

"Go ahead," says Margot, seeing now on the clock that is just past five-thirty. She was asleep for a few hours. "I'm going to wait till after rush hour. Poke around a little bit."

"Drive safe, then," Chad says. "Love you."

"Love you, too," says Margot and hangs up the phone. In the mirror she dislikes herself, eyes red from the crying, clothes a wrinkled mess from the rain and then sleeping in the bed.

She hurries into the shower, and while the water tumbles over her she thinks about this, the boring safety of marriage, how moments ago she was just a woman in a hotel room, asleep, and now she is racing to put herself back together to get home to her husband, who will have eaten his Thai food out of a box in front of *SportsCenter*, having fulfilled his obligation for calling her and now grateful for her absence, since he can spend this time alone after his flight.

In the mirror she applies her makeup. When she is finished, she stares at her reflection and makes small corrections here and there. Margot looks now like someone who spent a day shopping in New York, and she suddenly remembers she should e-mail Cricket and say they had a drink together when they didn't, but then she realizes that she would rather invite Chad's questions than Cricket's. Plus, what are the odds of Chad even saying something?

Instead, sitting on the edge of the bed with her bag packed, a bag she will have to hide in the way back of her SUV, as if she has not been away for a few days, she pulls out the business card Henry gave her earlier today.

She texts his number into the phone and then writes, "It was good to see you today. Oh, this is Margot."

Then she hits SEND and holds her breath.

A reply is back in moments. "It was GREAT to see you."

Oh, Jesus, Margot thinks, her heart racing. She has a sudden urge to be outside, to run again. Don't think, she tells herself. She types quickly with her thumbs. "We should do it again sometime. Maybe not on the street."

"Meet me for a drink. Not tonight. I have Jess. But Monday."

Margot sits and stares at his sentences on her phone. She feels somehow as if she has already cheated, like she won't be able to look Chad in the eye when he rises out of his chair to give her a perfunctory hug.

But for the first time in a long time, she doesn't really give a shit, and this is a good feeling. It has been forever since she has done something that feels true and honest.

She types back. "Where?"

A moment later, her phone lights up again.

"Anywhere you are willing to be," the poet says.

Henry, 1991

Now this: coming to, bright sun through the doorway, a pounding in his temples from the wine the night before, an awareness that she is not next to him anymore, sentience returning like a migraine, sitting up and then thinking it might be a miracle to stand, wondering what time it is, when he hears raised voices from outside the cabin.

Henry stands and quickly puts on a pair of jeans and pulls on a T-shirt. Holy shit, his head aches. Then the voices from outside are louder now, a man's voice and then, clearly, Margot's, unintelligible through the walls but sounding distressed.

Henry is an animal, hangover be damned, the former shortstop, still quick as a cat, out the door and into blinding morning sunlight, which obscures even the blue sky the way it beats down directly on the east side of the cabin.

It is disorienting for a moment, but then coming around the corner, he sees them, Margot and some man, and at first he thinks it must be Ted, the vitner, for who else could be here?

But the man is taller than Ted, and as Henry moves toward where the two of them are standing across from each other, not aware that he is only some twenty yards away, he sees Margot push the man hard in the chest, and then the man reaches for her, in almost a hug, and turns her around, brings her in tight to him, the way someone would subdue a violent child. He is hurting her.

Henry runs into the sun. Around him, it all explodes like stars inside a dream. Margot's voice is distant, though she is right there. The man's jaw is a fat fastball down the middle. Henry's almost leaping in the air as he punches him as hard as he can, and then it's all terribly wrong as the man goes down.

Margot yells no in that half second before he swings; then she goes down to the ground next to the man while the pain shoots from Henry's fist up his arm. The man is prone on the ground. His hands hold his face. Thankfully, his legs are moving.

The madness leaves Henry quick as a fever. Margot is saying "Dad" over and over again.

Oh fuck oh fuck oh fuck, what has he done?

Henry goes toward them and Margot turns from where she is bent down and sees him and says, "Get away from me!"

Henry steps back, and for a while he just paces around barefoot, his hands in his hair. Then Ted is there and it is so surreal: Time has stopped. Margot's father is on his feet. He is being led away by Ted and Margot.

Thirty minutes later, the police are there, a man and a woman from the sheriff's office. The conversation is brief. He has broken a man's jaw. How does he feel about that?

He's lucky he's not being arrested for murder, the female cop says. A punch like that can kill a man.

Henry doesn't try to explain. He looks away from the sun and to the lake, where the steeples of Bannister College can be seen, ancient turrets rising up over the hills on the western side.

"I'm sorry," he says. "I am so sorry."

They cuff Henry's hands behind his back. And as they take him away in the car to Seneca Falls, he looks out the window at the passing cornfields that line the rural highway, their tassels nodding slightly in the warm summer breeze, placid witnesses to what he has done.

Henry, 1991

After he is processed, they take Henry in back to one of the two cells in the sheriff's office. They allow him to make his phone call and he struggles with whom to call. It certainly isn't going to be his parents; just the thought of the two of them trying to figure out what to do from so far away, he can't imagine.

So Henry calls Deborah Weinberg, his poetry professor, and an hour later she is there with her husband, who teaches comparative literature and whom Henry knows mainly in passing. As they sit in wheeled-in office chairs across from where he is behind bars, he explains it is as best as he can, that he didn't know it was Margot's father, Thomas Fuller, but thought it was some stranger assaulting her. Oh, if he could have that moment back.

"Wait," Deborah's husband, David, says in his soft voice. "Thomas Fuller? From the board of trustees?"

Henry nods.

"Jesus," David says.

Deborah shoots her husband a look. "First things first," she says. "We need to get you out of here."

"They said I am going in front of a judge today," says Henry.

"You need a lawyer," David says.

"They're giving me one, I guess."

"We know somebody," Deborah says.

That afternoon, Henry meets with his lawyer, a disheveled older man with the remarkable name of Rudolph Holmes. His office is on Main Street in the town of Bannister and he specializes in Bannister students in trouble.

"I don't have any money for a lawyer," Henry says.

"Deborah and Dave are taking care of it," Rudolph says.

Henry bows his head, for the kindness humbles him and he doesn't want it, but he also knows he has no choice.

The hearing itself lasts all of ten minutes once it is his turn. It is all a soupy mirage. They rise and move to the tables at the front. There is some kind of announcement that precedes this, which Henry hears as background noise. The woman before him, clearly pregnant, gets sentenced to forty-five days for bouncing checks. Henry tries to figure this out. When she will have the baby?

Henry listens to Rudolph Holmes saying it was all a mistake and that this is a good kid with no priors, a straight-A student, you understand, who thought he was protecting his girlfriend. What person would have done different? And, by the way, there is no history of violence or mental illness.

"A good kid, Your Honor," Rudolph Holmes says, and then he sits down.

The judge, a small dark-haired woman with thick glasses, looks over at Henry and then back to the assistant district attorney. A few minutes later, he is outside, having been released on his own recognizance and into the custody of the Weinbergs, distinguished professors and unassailable citizens of Bannister.

David pats him on the back as he climbs into the back of their Prius and then they take him on the same drive the sheriff took him on earlier, though in reverse. In the bright sun, they pass the cornfields, and then the road opens up and he can see the entirety of the lake stretching south toward Watkins Glen.

They pull down the long driveway to the winery, and when they come around the final loop through the vines to where it opens to a small sandy parking lot, Ted is waiting there, as if expecting them, and next to him are Henry's two duffel bags. He hadn't thought this far until now, but it is all he needs to know, and David and Deborah don't even turn off the engine of the car as he gets out and walks over to Ted.

Ted looks at him and says, "You understand I don't have a choice."

"I know," says Henry.

Ted lifts the bags and hands them to Henry. Henry stares at Ted for a moment and then Ted nods, as if there is nothing else to say, and Henry knows this is true.

David and Deborah take Henry back to their house, a

two-story redwood house designed by Cornell architecture students, deep in a wooded lot a mile east of campus. On the way there, they drive through the heart of Bannister College, past the brick dorms and the great stone buildings. Henry has never seen it like this before, practically empty without any students, only a solitary figure visible here and there on the pathways that are normally bustling with young men and women, backpacks slung over their shoulders.

That night, Deborah makes up a bed for Henry in the guest room. The house is like nothing Henry has ever seen before, a great room of wide-plank redwood at the center of it, with bookshelves that extend from the floor to the ceiling, and two ladders on rails for access to the higher books. It might be the most beautiful thing Henry has ever seen, and looking around that room—that library—with something approaching wonder, Henry even forgets the events of the day for a moment.

But after a dinner of grilled lamb chops, a salad, bread, and much wine, it rushes back to him. Deborah says he should feel free to stay with them as long as he likes, and they don't mention the very real possibility that he might be going away for a while in a few weeks when he returns to court.

"I'm going to go home tomorrow," Henry announces.

"To Providence?" David asks.

"Yes," Henry says. "I don't know what else to do."

Deborah reaches across the table and puts her hand on his. "You will get through this, you know?"

Henry nods. "I hope so," he says, and as soon as he says it, he realizes he isn't thinking about the possibility of prison, or whether Bannister will let him back in, and he isn't thinking about his future at all, which just a day ago seemed as clear and as promising as mountain water.

Instead, the only thing he can think of is Margot, and right now there is a hole in his heart, where earlier in the same day she used to live.

After Deborah and Dave retire to their bedroom with their books and cups of tea, Henry picks up the phone in the kitchen and dials information and asks for a number for Thomas Fuller on Martha's Vineyard.

"I have one in Chilmark," the operator says. "Hold for the number."

A woman answers the phone on the third ring. "Hello?"

"Is Margot there?"

There is a moment of silence. Then the woman says, "I know who this is. If you ever call here again, I will call the police. Do you understand?"

"I just really need to talk to Margot," Henry says. "Please."

There is a click and then Henry is left listening to the metronomic emptiness of a dial tone.

Margot, 1991

Her mother hangs up the phone in the kitchen. Margot has drifted in, having heard it ring, and is there long enough to know who was on the other end of the line. And long enough for her mother to know that she knows who was on the other end of the line.

"Clarity is important here," her mother says. "You know that."

Margot nods. She is feeling oddly grown-up and responsible suddenly, though perhaps that is just indicative of how eternal this day has been. She thinks of her father at Mass General in Boston, refusing to be treated anywhere else, the speeding drive to the airport in Syracuse and then Kiernan instructing the pilot to take them to Boston. Her father, following surgery, stuck with his jaw wired shut and her knowing that this man who has made all his money peddling sugar water around the globe will be on a diet for more than a month, when all he will be able to take are liquids. The very virility cut out of him as easily as a knife slices into a peach. And that Henry was the one who did it.

"It was my fault, really," her mother is saying. "I never should have let you go up there. I mean, who goes upstate in the summer?"

Margot tunes her mother out. She feels now like she might be sick, the hangover, the wine from the night before in a place that feels like a world away, the whirlwind drive to the airport, the two plane flights, first to Boston, where her father was taken to Mass General, and then refueling the Gulfstream before it took her alone to the Vineyard, where her mother was waiting for her.

Maybe, though, it is her mother who is nauseating her. Her mother in her pink Izod with the collar turned up, her gold necklaces and rings and bracelets, her white capri pants snug on her ample ass and the overwhelming floral smell of her, turned up to hide the cigarette she had an hour ago, which Margot still faintly smells, like the sad undertone of sex in a motel room.

She then thinks of Henry, and suddenly her stomach is churning with the stress of it all. She remembers Kiernan making the call from the Town Car on the way to the airport and then his turning to her while her father held his face in his hands in the backseat.

"You can forget him," he said. "He's going to prison."

Now her mother is prattling on, and the bile is rising in her throat. Margot cannot hear her anymore, just empty maternal blather, and now she knows she is about to throw up, and she moves as quickly as she can to the bathroom off the kitchen and gets there just in time to have the vomit land in a torrent in the toilet bowl.

"Christ, Margot," her mother says behind her. "You're not one of those bulimics, are you? A lot of the girls are, I hear."

Margot is about to answer her when she dry-heaves. Emptied, she spins her head toward her mother. "No, I am not."

"I mean, it's okay if you are."

"Mom, no. I'm hungover. I got drunk last night. I should have done this hours ago."

"Okay, dear. I just meant you *can* tell me."

Margot simply glares at her and stands up and straightens herself out in the mirror. She desperately wants to be outside now, like these walls are closing in all around her, and she has a pang of memory as she remembers last night amid the vines, the dewy grass against her pants and the feel of Henry on top of her.

"I'm going for a walk," she says to her mother.

"Do you want me to come with you?"

"No, I really just want to be alone."

Margot goes through the French doors and out onto the patio and then past the curated landscape and through the narrow path between the half-moons of dunes and onto the beach. The sand is soft and deep here, and she takes off her sandals and holds them in her right hand as she leaves the dunes behind and walks out on the broader beach.

Once she is away from the protection of the dunes, the wind

picks up and blows her hair back and presses her clothes against her body. The beach is empty. Where the ocean meets the sand, the surf slaps hard against it over and over.

Looking up at the expanse of ocean stars, Margot finds it hard to imagine it is the same day. That a single day, one rotation of the planet, can contain an abundance of lives, the way the sky can contain stars that stretch and curve away from her toward Europe somewhere far out beyond the blackness.

She remembers then a night—could it have been a week ago?—when she sat outside the small cabin near the lake with Henry. They sat cross-legged on the grass with a bottle of wine open and he had his arm around her waist and they looked up at the sky, the same sky she is looking at right now, almost as pronounced, though the black of the ocean at night does something to draw the stars even closer than they were under those open fields.

She remembers looking over at Henry and in the dark his face was tilted toward the firmament, the wide gauzy stripe of the Milky Way, and the expression he wore was one she recognized and loved, half wonder and half amusement and just pure poetry, his mind spinning like a clock, rotating and whirring as he took in the possibilities.

"What do you see?" she asked.

"They're fucking amazing, aren't they?"

"The stars?"

"Yes," he said. "Do you think if we could see the backs of them, they would look the same?"

"The backs of them?"

"Yes," Henry said. "The backs of the stars."

Margot shook her head. "How do you come up with this stuff?"

He didn't answer with words. He just turned and kissed her.

Now, looking up at the great ineffable beyond, she listens to the crashing of the waves, and she walks on the sand hardened by the endless beat of the swells, and the hard truth that she will never see Henry again, can never see Henry again, rolls over her, heavy and unyielding as the surf.

Henry, 1991

The inside of a Greyhound bus might be the saddest place in America. It is, Henry thinks, looking out the window, the old dirty dog of its name cutting through the ugly seam of an otherwise-beautiful country.

He has thirteen days until his next court appearance. David dropped him at the bus station in Syracuse after Henry resisted their pleas just to stay with them, and now he is streaming down the interstate on a gray, rainy day. Henry looks around the bus. It is half-empty. Some are sleeping. A few are reading. Some, like him, stare blankly out at the flat landscape, as if somewhere out there are answers to whatever question has them traveling this lonely stretch of road on this particular day.

With the myriad of stops, a trip he could drive in six hours becomes double that, and by the time he finally steps off the bus in Providence, it is dark out. His parents don't know he is coming. He debated calling them, but his mother is not good on the phone—it makes her hyper, every word a small emergency—and his father looks at the phone when it rings as if he is seeing it for the first time.

Instead, he just walks the eight blocks home, his duffel bags slung heavily over each shoulder. He is exhausted and hungry. Soon he is away from downtown and back in the old hood, and it looks even shabbier in the dark than he remembered, the paint peeling off the triple-deckers visible in the light from the streetlamps. He has also forgotten the smells, coming past the diner with its vent out to the sidewalk, the overwhelming smell of old frying oil, and the sounds, too, the raised voices, a "Hey, fucking Johnny, get back here" shouted out into the night from a third-floor apartment.

And in this way, Henry arrives at the house, the apartment, he grew up in. It is just past nine at night and he can picture, before he even walks up those three flights of stairs, the scene inside. His mother is flitting around the kitchen, the dishes already done, but making herself busy. His father sits in front of the television, the Red Sox game on if he can get it, an old movie if he cannot, a can of Coke in his hand.

Henry takes a deep breath. And then he climbs the stairs, aware of every creak from the thin wood, his footsteps a foreshadowing of the profound failure he is about to present to the two people he least wants to present it to.

When he reaches the door, he can peer past the curtain on the door window, and it is as he expected: There is his mother in her customary black, moving around the kitchen, and from here even he can hear the roar of the television in the other room. Henry knocks and he sees his mother stop, her eyes narrow as she turns toward the door.

When she opens it, he stands there for a moment and then drops his bags.

"Oh, Henry," she says. "What? Why are you here?"

Henry steps forward and holds out his arms. His mother hugs him. With his hands, he can feel the curvature of the spine that will grow more conspicuous over time, until she is one of those women who are permanently stooped over. But for now he just holds his mother and she holds him until she leads him inside to the small table in the kitchen.

"Karl," his mother shouts. "Henry is here."

"I'm hungry," Henry says.

"Let me fix you something."

And like that, adulthood melts like ice. His mother is at the fridge for the eggs, and then is stirring them with a fork. A pan warms on the stove. His father is suddenly filling the doorframe, giving a nod, as if he understands something has happened.

"Dad," Henry says, and goes to him for a handshake that becomes the awkward half hug they have figured out over time.

As Henry eats his eggs and the dark bread his mother makes every morning with the same dedication that she gives to her three daily prayers, he reluctantly warms to his story. Both his parents sit, his father to his left, his mother right in front of him at the small table. His mother's dark eyes are on him as he tells what happened, and he cannot look at her, for he does not want to see her disappointment, her fear of a life upended, so he looks from his father to the kitchen beyond him, as if seeing it anew, the way the linoleum peels up in the corners under the metal cupboards.

His mother has a million questions, and he tries to answer them. What does it all mean? Is he going to jail? What about college? How did you get mixed up with this terrible girl?

His father breaks his own silence and says, "You come to work with me tomorrow."

"Yes," says Henry.

And so early the next morning, Henry finds himself alongside his father in empty office buildings, running machines over hard floors, washing and polishing them in great circles. The work is a palliative, for between the whirl of the machines and the simplicity of it all—see, move, and then circle—Henry finds he has no room in his mind except for what is in front of him. Looking over at his father, his earphones on, too, and alone in his own world, he finds a sudden and great comfort in why he has always enjoyed this work. The practical labor of it, and the idea that you can always see the finish line, unlike a poem, which famously is never finished and can only abandoned.

And maybe, Henry thinks, this is where he was meant to be all along, the rest of it all some crazy lark, as if he accidentally fell down the rabbit hole and ended up in a place he had no business being in the first place.

But then at night, alone on the porch after both his parents have gone to bed, it comes on him fast as a fever and he wonders if his life has shrunk back to the dimensions he was always meant to inhabit.

But in defiance, he thinks, No, this is not possible. Margot is more real, not less, than anything that has ever happened to him. How can he deny the heaviness in his heart that takes his breath away?

And on that ragged porch, he sometimes looks into the kitchen, where the phone hangs from the wall, the same phone his mother used to answer when he made his calls from Bannister. And Henry considers going to pick it up and dialing that number on the Vineyard again, hoping Margot answers and that he can plead with her, but then he remembers her mother's voice on the other end of the line.

It occurs to him one night that Margot has no idea where he is and probably assumes he is still at the winery. Perhaps she has tried to reach him there, and so he calls Ted and Laura's number, even though he knows it is late. It is Laura who answers on the third ring, and he can tell from her sleepy voice that he has intruded on their lives once again.

"I'm sorry to bother you, Laura," he says. "Has Margot called there?"

"No, Henry. No one has called."

In the mornings, his mother makes lunches for both Henry and his father, and before dawn they are at it, cleaning and cleaning and cleaning. The day ends at noon, and one afternoon Henry tells his father he will see him at home, and then he walks out through these office buildings they have been working on, through these low-slung industrial buildings that sit on the edge of where the Providence River runs to the sea. Around him, men on forklifts move giant pallets of something, and he passes them until he reaches the seawall.

The day is warm, with bright sun, and a breeze rolls off the bay and pushes Henry's hair back as he sits down on the seawall and dangles his legs over the dark, brackish water. Looking off in the distance, he can see where the open ocean is, and somewhere out there is Martha's Vineyard, so close, yet entirely distant from him. He tries to imagine Margot on the island, and he wonders if she sits as he does, perhaps on the beach, looking toward the mainland and thinking about him.

After a while, Henry stands up and wanders home. He walks through the old neighborhood, and a few of the typical characters shout to him and he greets them with a wave. Down a small side street, he passes a stickball game in progress, and since he is not in a rush to go back to the small apartment, he stops and watches it for a while, boys hitting a tennis ball with a broomstick as he once did, and for a moment the sight truly pleases him, the exaggerated windups of the pitchers, the ball whipping toward the brick wall that has home plate drawn on it as a white square in chalk. He watches a skinny brown-skinned kid with a mop of curly hair square one up and pull it, the tennis ball flying high into the air and landing on a rooftop, a home run. The hoots and hollers that follow it bring a smile to Henry's face.

When Henry finally returns home, it is late afternoon. He is halfway up the rickety outdoor staircase when he hears voices coming through the screen door of the family apartment. One is his mother's and the other is not his father's. Henry goes quickly up the stairs, and when he reaches the door, he hears his mother say, "Here is Henry."

Henry opens the metal screen door and steps into the warm kitchen. The door slaps closed behind him. Both his mother and father are on one side of the table and on the other is a tall, squared-jawed man who looks to be in his thirties. He wears a pale blue suit and shiny light brown shoes.

The man stands up, but he doesn't smile. He extends his hand, though, and he says with an accent that sounds vaguely British, "I'm Kiernan Meyer."

Henry takes the man's hand and looks quickly to his parents and then back up to the man. He is easily six foot five and broad.

Henry is about to speak when it is as if Kiernan anticipates what he is about to say and says, "I work for Mr. Thomas Fuller and I am here on his behalf."

"What do you want?" Henry says.

"Sit down, please," Kiernan says.

Henry looks toward his father, that impassive and unknowing face, and then to his mother, who of course tells him what he needs to do with a nod and with the stern look in her black eyes. She says, "Sit down, Henry."

Henry sits in the closest chair, and next to him Kiernan

eases himself into a matching chair, a chair too small for his folded body, like a parent visiting an elementary school classroom.

"Henry," Kiernan says, "I've had a chance to talk with your parents. But you need to hear what I am going to say. It's important. Do you understand? Are you listening?"

Henry shrugs. "I'm listening," he says.

"These are the facts, okay? You assaulted a man and broke his jaw. No one disputes that. The fact that he is a very important man does not matter in terms of what the court will do, except that perhaps we could be helpful to you. From talking to the prosecutor, I would say you could be looking at a year in prison. Prison, Henry, understand?"

Henry nods as his mother gasps loudly, and he can hear her start to cry, but he cannot look at her. Instead, he looks only at Kiernan, who has gray eyes, and his head is so large that when he looks at Henry, it unnerves him, and while he is hearing him, he also desperately wants him to go, or to have this conversation somewhere where his parents cannot hear it.

"I have also talked to President Matthews at Bannister. They are prepared to move forward with an expulsion hearing for violating the code of conduct, which applies equally to off-campus activities. So right now you are looking at being kicked out of Bannister and a year in prison."

Kiernan pauses as if to let this news settle in. His mother is crying harder now, and Henry finally looks over to her and says, "It's going to be okay, Mom. Really."

"Well, it could be," says Kiernan. "Mr. Fuller is very forgiving man. And so against my advice, he has asked me to come here today to give you an opportunity to get your life back on track."

"Why?" Henry asks.

"I'll get to that in a minute. The prosecutor, at Mr. Fuller's recommendation, is prepared to give you probation without any time, provided you agree to the following. First, you will not return to Bannister, but you will be allowed to graduate. President Matthews says you have met all your distribution requirements, so the work left is all in your major, creative writing. Professor Deborah Weinberg has agreed to advise you in the production of a thesis that will be a substitute for normal coursework. You can do the work from here or anywhere else, but you will not be allowed back on the Bannister campus for a period of five years. If you successfully complete the thesis, your transcript will not reflect any detriment to you."

Henry takes this in. He looks around the kitchen and then out the small window that stares at the identical house next door, and for a moment, incongruently, he thinks about this, houses next to houses, all of them the same other than their colors, many of which were once garish but now are dulled by time, like so many things.

"What's the catch?" Henry's father says from across the table, shaking Henry back to what is in front of him. "There's always a catch."

"Just an agreement," Kiernan says. "Henry will agree not

to contact Margot Fuller ever again. And Henry will write her a letter now, to be approved by me and mailed by me, that will explain to her that he is not interested in seeing her again and this is of his free will. He will tell her he has left Bannister College. And should he try to contact her in any manner in violation of this, or inform her in any way of this agreement, it all goes away. He will be expelled from Bannister. He will be tried and convicted. A stain he will carry for the rest of his life. And given the gravity of what has happened, he will go to prison. Is this clear?"

Henry stands up quickly, the metal legs of the chair scraping against the floor. He pushes his hands through his hair. His mother, ever the survivor, is saying something to Kiernan. Henry is not listening to her, though he knows she is expressing some measure of gratitude, for his mother always sees the horizon. It is what got her here and what has kept her here.

Henry opens the screen door and moves out into the warmth of the stale summer afternoon.

Margot, 1991

All the simple things about summer that used to please her don't matter anymore. Things she used to love, like the washing of sticky sand off her feet in the surf and the feeling of putting a clean white shirt on after a day on the white-hot beach, the way it tingles against her tanned skin, are suddenly irritants. She doesn't want to see anyone. And the sight of her father sitting all day on the deck, hat over his eyes, with his big glass and the straw, the visible wires holding his face together, his sustenance reduced to this, reminds her of the moment love crashed into the sun.

Otherwise, it is like this thing never happened. They have one conversation about it when her father returns, and Margot bites her tongue, for she wants to tell him what she has realized, that Henry did what he did only to protect her, and wouldn't they want her involved with a man like that?

Of course, it is more complicated than that, and she knows

it. Her parents will never actually say it, but to Margot, it is clear that they believe they had no business being together, and it is not lost on Margot that, yes, this is about money, but it is also about the fact that he is a Jew, for this is the thing about the truly wealthy: Old prejudices fade slowly.

All Margot wants to do is stay in her room. She wants to sleep, but the sleep doesn't come easily, so she lies in her bed and in her mind she turns over all the time she spent with Henry, and just as she once thought she could never love another person with this kind of intensity, she also didn't know it was possible to grieve with this kind of intensity. The anger gives way to abject sadness, and despite the coaxing of her mother, she doesn't want to eat, doesn't want to play, doesn't want to swim in the ocean or go to the many parties the idle rich kids hold at the place where the beach meets the tidal river most every evening.

It is as if she has forgotten how to crave anything at all, and she wonders if it will ever be possible to be whole again.

One morning, Margot lies in her bed, her head pressed between two pillows, when a loud knocking comes at the door.

"Honey," her mother says. "May I come in?"

"Go away," Margot grumbles, though she sits up and rubs her eyes. What time is it? she wonders. Bright sun streams through the windows.

"You have mail," her mother says.

"Come in," Margot says.

The door swings open and her mother marches in and

comes over to the bed. She hands her a letter. "I thought you might want this."

Margot takes it from her and, seeing the handwriting, she is suddenly wide-awake and yet dreaming at the same time. She wants to peel it open, but not in front of her mother. She looks at her mom and says, "Can you leave?"

"Of course," her mother says, and then departs.

Margot opens the seal with her fingernail and reaches in and pulls out the folded piece of paper. And there in Henry's precise handwriting, it says:

Dear Margot,

I tried to call, but I don't really know what to say. I am sorry for what happened. I didn't know it was your father—I thought you were being hurt, and I couldn't allow that to happen. It was like I lost my mind and then it was over.

I would be lying if I didn't say I miss you like I miss spring in the middle of a snowstorm. But I also am a realist and try to be as practical as a poet can ever be.

It is clear to me that something changed between us that morning. Maybe everything changed. And that we can never have back whatever we had for the time that we had it. We don't belong together, I realized, and this is harsh to say, but it is true, and I know you know it as well as I do. I just felt the need to say it.

Whatever happens as a result of that day, I now know two things to be true. First is that I won't be returning to Bannister. I don't know what I will be doing, but I will never be there again. It has too many memories for me, and I don't belong there, either.

The second thing I know is that I won't be seeing you again. That pains me to no end, and maybe it doesn't pain you because you have already decided the same thing, but in case you haven't, it's the right thing for both of us.

I have had time now to think about all of this and I am clear-minded about it. I don't love you anymore. And suspect you don't love me. It is time for us to move forward with our lives and forget, as much as we can, that this ever happened. I wish you all the best.

Love,
Henry

Margot stops reading. And then, as if she didn't understand it, she reads it again. And then she lets out something like a yell, though different, more of a primitive yawp, and then slumps over on her bed and begins to cry.

She doesn't leave her room that entire day. But the next morning, she comes down and without a word to her parents or her sister, she walks the entire length of the beach. The sky above her is mottled with clouds and a strong wind is coming from the south, and as she walks, the surf is higher than usual, the kind that at the public beaches on the other side of the island they would post warnings about. It is just what she needs. The sound of it tumbling over and over is almost deafening, and as she walks, she feels it all begin to lift off her,

Henry, her father, all of it. The way she was raised to deal with matters like this. The sea somehow gives her a sense of her own capability to get through things.

That night after dinner, Margot is up in her room when her sister, Katherine, comes in.

"Hey," Katherine says, and Margot is reminded of how little they do this, how much they have been avoiding each other, when as children they were inseparable. It pangs her a little to think of how growing older often means growing apart.

"Hi," Margot says as Katherine sits down on the edge of her bed.

"I just wanted to say I am sorry about what happened," Katherine says.

"It's okay."

"No, I mean it. You remember when I was dating Doug? Then found out he slept with Anne out on the boat?"

Margot nods. She remembers Doug, and that summer, and she thinks that the situation has nothing in common with her and Henry, and this is what she came to terms to with this morning, the fact that no one will ever understand, that despite what anyone can say about heartache being universal, the truth is that it is entirely particular, too. It is entirely relative.

"Well, I thought I might die after that," Katherine says. "But then it got better. And I forgot all about it. Listen: Come out tonight. The Jones boys are doing a bonfire. Everyone is going to be there."

"I don't know," Margot says. "Don't you ever get tired of it? Smoking pot and drinking beer and Ian playing Grateful Dead songs on the guitar?"

"Why does everything have to be so serious? I think they're fun," Katherine says. "Come on. Get dressed. You're coming with me."

"Fine," Margot says.

And so on a night when the ocean stars look close enough to touch, Margot walks the length of the beach and back into the universe she was born into but for the past year had left. Out of the back of a jeep, the Jones boys have tapped a keg, and a driftwood fire burns high and bright. On the sand around it, they sit in small circles, and stories are told loudly, and cigarettes and joints are smoked, guitar is played, and there is singing. And perhaps Katherine is right: Why does everything have to be serious? It feels suddenly like a long time since Margot has let go, and with the beer and the simple comfort of the crackling fire, for the first time it is as if her mind, all the ideas that have consumed her, has been wiped free.

At one point, Chad, a boy she had kissed summers before, comes over and sits down next to her. He takes his plastic cup full of beer and leans it against hers.

"Cheers," he says.

Chad is a senior at Colby now, tall and blond, and someone she has known since she was in elementary school. His father develops golf courses around the world and their parents are friendly. He is handsome in a conventional way, but never really her type, too embedded, as he has been, in the fabric of all she has wanted to run away from, but tonight in the light from the fire, she likes the way his hair falls over his forehead, the brightness of his sharp blue eyes, the strength of his jaw. And later, when he suggests a walk, she knows what this means and she goes willingly, and when a half mile down the beach he stops and turns to her, Margot is the one who kisses him, stepping up on her tiptoes to meet his lips.

This is the forgetting she wants. It is her idea to get a blanket from her house, and down among the dunes, Margot lets Chad inside her. The sex itself is indifferent and lacks the urgency and the closeness she always had with Henry, but sometimes there are simple needs, and she wants to feel his weight on her, his breath on her neck, and as he moves on top of her, she looks beyond him to the infinite, placid sea of stars and tries to imagine he is not really there at all.

Henry, 2012

This is absurd, Henry thinks, standing in front of the full-length mirror in his small bedroom, tucking his button-down shirt into his jeans before untucking it, smoothing it down, and then spending another moment patting down his hair, looking at himself from every possible angle. He has tried on two pairs of jeans and two shirts and he hasn't left the apartment yet and he has already had two glasses of wine just to calm his nerves. He is far too old for this shit.

At 6:45, Henry leaves his apartment building. The night is hot and this is the season when he least likes the city—or loves, he should say, since despite everything else he has always loved the city, its wide avenues, its energy, and its graceful anonymity. But despite all that, the city magnifies everything, and especially the heat of a summer day, the way it radiates off the asphalt, and especially the stink of the black bags full of garbage piled around streetlamp poles.

Henry is later than he expected. Usually he would walk to Columbus Circle from here, for he has chosen Marea, an Italian seafood place that is a little pricey for him normally, but his challenges with his sartorial choices have put him behind, and also he is concerned this heat is going to have him sweating through his shirt. He can already feel it on his brow.

On Broadway, Henry hails a cab, and five minutes later he is standing in front of the restaurant, several hundred yards from where, earlier in the season, he saw Margot bend down next to a fallen bird.

Henry doesn't know what to do. He remembers suddenly the first time he walked into a classroom as an assistant professor, some fifteen years ago. How insanely nervous he felt, as if five minutes in, the students would realize he was a fraud and had no right to be the sage at the front of the workshop table, guiding them on how to do this thing that he had come to regard as pure madness, shaping ideas on paper, but yet something that he felt brought him as close as he could be to touching God.

Come to think of it, that experience pales compared to this one. Henry peers into the window of the restaurant and scans the bar and the waiting area as best he can. Should he wait for Margot inside or stand here on the street instead? What is the protocol here?

He decides to stay outside, but moves away from the doorway to the restaurant. Next to it is an exclusive apartment building, and in front of it the doormen chatter endlessly in their own particular patois, one that he loves—what they say when no one is listening. There are four of them, and from the look of them, they all come from different corners of the world but have this remarkable ability to keep a constant stream of banter going about cars and women and all kinds of things until that moment when someone is about to exit the building, and then they are suddenly formal and polite. They straddle two worlds, something Henry long ago learned a few things about.

As Henry is considering this, he sees Margot. She is walking from the circle in a throng of people and she has not seen him yet. She wears dark jeans and a light blouse, high brown boots. A brown bag is slung over her shoulder. She looks down as she walks. The look on her face is strained, and he wonders for a moment if she is aware of it, but then she looks up and she sees him and a broad smile comes over her face and he smiles back. Isn't it funny how easy we pick each other out from a crowd?

"Hi," Henry says when she is in front of him, and he can tell immediately from the flush in her face that she is as unhinged as he is about this meeting. She moves in for a hug and he, for a moment, takes her in his arms, though it is brief. Her perfume, subtle, smells vaguely of flowers.

"Hi," Margot says. "This is the place?" she asks, as if searching for something to say.

"Yes, I hope it's okay. Do you eat fish? It's kind of famous for fish. I should have asked."

She laughs. "I love fish."

"Oh, good. Shall we?"

"Please."

They are inside then, in front of a desk manned by a smiling older man surrounded by young, comely black-haired women in small black dresses that he dare not look at, and Henry is happy to have something to do, so practical this all is now, and yes, they have a reservation, and oh, a few minutes before the table is ready, and perhaps a seat at the bar?

"Thank you," Henry says.

They move to the bar. They are strangers. They are a couple. They are people who used to know each other. They are nothing. They are everything.

Margot slides onto an empty stool. Henry slips onto the one next to her and studies the bar. No one is staring at them, and that feels miraculous. Around them are couples meeting after work and thick-bodied businessmen with their blocky watches and their dark suits. The beauty of a bar is that everyone looks ahead at the array of bottles on glass shelves and seldom at one another. The city. Anonymity.

"Start you with drinks?" the bartender is saying.

"Hendrick's martini," Margot says. "Up. Olives."

"Same," says Henry, though he rarely drinks gin.

Henry pivots his stool and now he is facing Margot. She looks at him and with a practiced gesture runs her hand over her hair. She smiles again, dimples spreading, the lines around her eyes the only suggestion that time has interfered, and if anything, she is more astounding to him than she ever was, ever could have been, some twenty-plus years ago in western New York. He thinks then of all of the things that have conspired against them, and all the things that have come together to lead to this moment. He looks into her eyes. The bartender, to his left, places their drinks down. But Henry cannot turn that way. My God, he thinks, she empties me.

"I can't believe this," he says.

"Me either," she says.

"I mean, look at us."

"We're old, you mean."

"No, no. We're not old. Are we?"

Margot laughs. "Yes, Henry, we are."

"Fuck. I hate that."

"Let's have a drink."

"Yes, let's."

They pivot back then to the bar in front of them and away from each other. Margot picks up her drink and brings it to Henry's, and she touches her delicate glass to his and says, "Cheers."

"Cheers," says Henry.

They raise their glasses to their mouths, and at that moment the older man from the front desk comes over to tell them their table is ready.

"Would you mind if we just stayed here?" Margot asks, and this relieves Henry, somehow less pressure to sit at the bar, to be able to face forward, as if they just happened upon each other.

"Of course," the man says.

Henry turns to Margot. "I don't know where to begin," he says.

She laughs. "Me either."

"I have a confession. I tried on three different outfits."

Margot smiles. "Well, you look very nice. And I have a confession, too. I tried on four."

"I was—I am—very nervous."

"I almost didn't come."

"Really?"

"Really. I thought about telling you I was sick."

Henry laughs. "What is wrong with us?"

"I have no idea."

The bartender is there then, wondering if they have questions about the menu. They pay attention to it for the first time, and for Henry it is all a blur; he is aware of the need to eat, that the gin is going to his head, but focusing on it is hard when all he can think about is that Margot is next to him, and what a strange thing life is, that you can actually reach across time like this and pluck someone out of the past as easily as a nectarine.

Margot says, "Oh, I can't. I eat everything. Can you order for us?"

And so Henry does. He hopes he is acting with coherence, but in truth his choices are random. And one by one dishes come out: shimmering raw crudo, octopus that has been marinated and sliced paper-thin, a pasta blackened with squid ink, and finally a whole branzino that the bartender in a theatrical show brings over to the two of them and displays—long and gray, with bright black marbles for eyes—before it is cooked in a salt crust and then brought back to them as flaky white fillets on a big white plate. He arrays a tray of sauces in front of them, and Henry doesn't hear a word he says when he describes each one in great detail. All he sees are the colors—red, purple, and the bright green of the first trees of spring.

Margot does most of the talking at first. He does not remember this about her, and wonders if it is something she has developed later in life. She tells him about her two children, her son at Wesleyan, and her daughter in boarding school, also in Connecticut. She describes her husband, who works on Wall Street, and how they pass each other like ships in the night. "What a weird time of life this," she says, "don't you think?

"Sometimes," Margot continues, "I think there has to be more to it. Do you know what I mean?"

"I do," says Henry.

"It's like everyone just goes so fast for so long and then you find yourself here and it's all so, I don't know, uneventful? Boring? That sounds awful. I don't mean that. I have been very blessed."

"I have a question," Henry says.

Margot looks him in the eyes. It amazes him that they can have this ease and comfort with each other after all these years, the give-and-take so natural, and he imagines she must feel the same way, for in her eyes he sees how he feels.

"What?" she says.

"How come you hid from me all these years?"

Margot sips from her gin and looks away, and she is aware

of her legs suddenly shaking and she is happy she is on a stool and that Henry cannot see this. She looks straight ahead when she speaks and her voice softens to almost a whisper.

"Everything I have done in my life is wrong," she says. "Everything."

"No, it doesn't work that way," Henry says. "Things happen, you know? All we can do is try our best. I am sure you have done that."

"I haven't," Margot says. "This is the thing I always loved about you. How generous you are. You always saw the best in me. And I didn't deserve it."

Henry sits with this for a moment. The bartender is there now, clearing the dinner plates. The restaurant has filled up all around them, stylishly dressed, wealthy people, and for a moment he thinks of the bill to come, and adding up in his head, he realizes it will probably be more than what he pays for food over several weeks and then he chastises himself for the pettiness of that thought. The restaurant suddenly feels close, though, and he wants to be outside with Margot, having this conversation illicitly in the dark.

When the bartender leaves, Henry says, "I never stopped loving you. Never. Not a day went by when somehow you didn't enter my thoughts. I am sorry. I needed to say that."

Margot takes her hand and brings it to his cheek. Her lips part as if she is going to say something, but he can see that her bottom lip is quivering. And in that moment there is no one else in that gilded, overwrought room, no one else at the zinc-topped bar, no one else moving down the avenue behind them.

"It's okay," Henry says. "Really. Let's get out of here."

The bill comes and Margot goes for her bag and Henry says, "No. I got it."

"Are you sure?"

"Yes," he says. "Please."

The evening kicks them out onto the uncaring sidewalk. With the sun having set, some of the heat has diffused, though it is humid.

"Do you have to go?" Henry asks.

Margot looks at her watch. "I have an hour or so," she says. "Before my husband starts to be curious."

They walk across the street to the entrance to the park. People are everywhere. Street artists are doing charcoal portraits. Horse-drawn carriages are lined up one after another, most of the drivers just sitting on their perches, others like carnival barkers, trying to get a fare. The horses seem sad and out of place, huge blinders shielding their eyes. And then at the mouth of the park, Margot suddenly cries out in delight. She takes his arm and points. "Look!"

And in front of them, a bright purple light shoots into the air, followed by another and another. The lights rise above the trees and then fall down slowly, fluttering. As they get closer, they realize there are dozens of young men shooting tiny lights into the air with long elastic bands. Hundreds of tiny falling stars, and it couldn't be more magical.

They find a bench and sit down and watch this spontaneous show. They don't talk. Margot sits close to Henry, her thigh almost touching his thigh.

"God, it's beautiful," she says.

"Yes," Henry says. "It really is."

Margot, 2012

They sit for a while in silence, watching the whimsical light show, and the silence is a different one for her, not the sad, empty silence of sitting across from Chad in a restaurant and struggling to find something to say. And maybe, Margot thinks, this is what love really is, the ability to be fully you with another person, to let all the carefully constructed veneers fall away and not have to think anymore, but just *be.*

She doesn't want the night to end anymore, the anxiety she had before having disappeared somewhere after the second martini, when it seems they decided to let their shared history disappear like the tiny piece of fish they forked off the plate. But in her mind, she has already scripted it out. She remembers then sitting on another bench a long time ago, also on a warm night, looking out over the lake in Bannister, New York. How young she was then, how eager to be a woman; how easy it was for her to make the first move, turning to

Henry and kissing him. And now she doesn't remember the last time she was kissed—really kissed, not the public peck or the kiss good night. How long has that kind of intimacy been closed to her?

Margot knows how tonight will end. It won't end with her waking up in his apartment, though she considered this. No, it will end with a kiss, out on the street in the hot summer night, the black Lincoln arriving when she makes her call, waiting to whisk her back to the suburbs, and her not wanting to let go of Henry.

And this is how it plays out. Riding out of the city in the backseat, she stares out the window at the passing buildings and soon they are on the Merritt and under the stone bridges, and the closer she gets to home, the emptier she feels, and she has to remind herself to pull it together before the car pulls down her tree-lined cul-de-sac and drops her in her driveway.

That night, after a quick hello to Chad, who barely looks up from the television—"How were the girls?" he asks; she says, "Oh, the usual"—she goes upstairs and draws herself a bath, and when she sinks into it, she doesn't know whether to cry or to smile, and she settles, as best she can, on the latter, and when she closes her eyes with the hot water swelling around her body, it is Henry she sees, of course, next to her at the restaurant bar, leaning in as he listens to her, as if every inane thing she had to say was somehow as new and original as a poem. And this is his gift, the gift of listening, and it reminds Margot how plenty of people know how to talk but precious few are good at listening.

The next day, Margot sleeps late. She is vaguely aware of Chad leaving in the morning, his routine, the half hour down on the treadmill, then his shower and his getting dressed in the walk-in closet as he does, going in wearing a towel and emerging like the Wall Street superhero he loosely aspires to be, a crisp suit and shiny brown shoes on. When she rolls back over a few hours later, he is gone.

Margot sits up in bed. Looking out the windows, she can see the day is overcast, though it doesn't appear to be raining. She reaches for her phone. She stares at it, looking for the text from Henry that is not there. What is the protocol here? Perhaps it's too old-fashioned to think he should be the one to reach out to her? Did she imagine the idea that time had done nothing to erode their connection? A barb of doubt comes over and she thinks, Oh, be grateful, will you? Do you want to throw everything away?

Margot looks out at the gray day and a wave of sadness sweeps over here. She suddenly longs for her children. Emma is deep in the woods of Maine, probably out on a canoe in the middle of the vast lake, or on one of the daily hikes they take to some vista where you can see hundreds of miles of green forests rolling toward the sea. Alex is in the city, like his father, his first job, though unpaid, and at a publisher, of all things. She remembers that conversation when he said he wanted to be an editor, and she was proud of Chad, for though he said he thought books were dying out in America, and that editors were lucky to make enough money to afford to live near the city, let alone in it, he also told Alex he thought he should take the position and see what he thought for himself. Of course, it was a far easier thing to say knowing that Alex would leave college with a healthy trust fund intact from his grandparents.

Margot takes her phone then and texts her son.

"Can you escape for coffee?" she writes.

The response comes immediately. "Yeah. U okay?"

"Fine. Just miss you."

An hour and half later, she waits for her tall son to emerge from the Flatiron Building. When he finally comes out, looking to her like such a full-fledged man in his coat and tie, the goofy flop of hair dangling over his forehead the only remnant of his teenage years, Margot feels something give within her. She goes to Alex and hugs him.

"You sure you're okay?" he says.

"Of course. Just wanted to see you. Are you too old now for your mother?"

"Jeez. No."

In front of them as they walk is the Empire State Building, the best view of it in the city, the great limestone obelisk rising up above the other buildings. At a Starbucks a block away, she orders both of them lattes. He doesn't have long before he needs to be back. He tells her about the work, mainly filing and running errands, sorting mail. But the other day, a famous author stopped by and everyone drank champagne to celebrate the delivery of her latest manuscript, a certain bestseller. Alex talks about how hot the building gets, up on the nineteenth floor, and the ancient and slow elevators. How in the dive apartment in Alphabet City that he shares with two other boys from college they sit at night in their underwear and drink beer in front of fans. And looking at her soft-eyed son, Margot finds herself getting nostalgic for the time of life he is occupying, and part of her hates herself for this, the always looking back, the inability to live now or for the future, and maybe, she thinks, this is what it means to be over forty. Everything interesting is behind you and you live out the string as best you can, finding the small moments that make you happy. Either that or start over.

Walking through Union Square Park by herself fifteen minutes later, Margot feels her phone vibrate, and the text that comes through makes her smile.

"Are you there?" Henry writes.

It is such a poet's question, Margot thinks. Does he mean am I out in the world somewhere? Or is it the more narrow question: Am I currently holding my phone in my hand?

"I am here," writes Margot.

Margot stops walking and stares at her phone. People stream around her. She moves into the lee of a building to escape them.

"I can't think of anything but you," Henry writes. "I just taught a class and I don't remember a thing about it. I need to see you. Can I come out there? Are you alone?"

"You don't have to come out," Margot types back. "I am here."

Henry, 2012

The funny thing about getting older, Henry decides, is how the rules you lived with for so long change. For much of his adult life, he wouldn't have dreamed of having a drink before five, that very rational marker that indicated the shift to nighttime. And often it was far later than that, for if he had work to do, he liked to address it with a clear head. Among his colleagues, this made him unusual.

And yet here he finds himself at a little past noon with an open bottle of wine across from Margot at a bistro near Union Square. He tops her glass off with the white wine and then pours himself another. He is feeling strong. Last night, he slept better than he had in a long time. The wine is helping. As are the french fries cooked in duck fat, which he eats with the relish of a teenager.

"I've had a night to think about this," Henry says. "Really think about it."

"What?"

"I'm going to Vermont in the morning. For a few days. I want you to come with me."

"Oh," Margot says. "I don't know. Where would I say I was going? I need to think."

Henry leans forward. "There are two places I feel like myself. Do you know what they are?"

Margot shakes her head. "No."

"This little cabin I bought on a lake in Vermont. And the second is with you. I need to know what happens if I put them both together. I need to know if it's all real."

"If what is real?"

Henry reaches into the side pocket of his messenger bag. "This," he says, and he hands a small rectangle to Margot.

"Oh," she says, and puts her hand over her mouth. It is a photograph, the only one he has of the two of them, and the sides of are wrinkled and it has a tear in it. It was taken on the Bannister campus, a sunny fall day. They are at the edge of the campus quad, on a small hillock, and he is sitting on the ground and smiling at the camera, while Margot looks up at his face adoringly.

"I can't believe you have this," she says.

"It's been much loved, like an old stuffed animal."

"Look at us," she says. "We were such babies."

"You know what's amazing to me?"

"What?"

"I think you are far more beautiful now."

"Oh, stop it. Really."

"No, I'm serious. All young people are kind of blandly beautiful, you know? Trust me. I teach them. But a measure of a woman's beauty is how she ages. And last night when I saw you coming down the street toward me, you took my breath away."

Henry sees the welling of tears in her eyes, and he says, "Hey, don't cry. It's okay."

Margot half laughs. "Then don't be so fucking nice to me."

"Will you come with me?"

"You know what is crazy? I've been married a long time and this doesn't feel wrong. What does that say about me?"

"Will you come?"

"Yes," Margot says. "Of course I will."

The next morning, on a clear, sunny day, Henry drives north out of the city, and off of I-95, he follows the sign for the train station in Stamford, and when he gets the parking lot, he drives through it, looking for her, and he doesn't see her anywhere. She decided not to come, he thinks. He drives around again. And then a moment later, a Mercedes SUV pulls into the lot, and even from this distance he can tell it is Margot. A moment later, she is parked and climbing into his Volkswagen with a small brown duffel bag.

"I didn't think you were going to come," Henry says.

"I'm just always late," she says. "You should know this about me. One of my many terrible qualities."

The weather holds all the way to Vermont. Three hours later, they are off the highway and driving those webs of half-marked dirt roads that lead to the lake. When they get to the final turn that is Henry's road, the cow path that cuts through the woods, he says, "We're here. And this is my favorite part. The road."

Up and through the trees they go, swooping down into the wide-open meadow before they are back into the woods again on the narrow dirt track, the dappled sunlight coming through the high trees and speckling the path in front of them. A minute later, the lake opens up in front of them and Henry looks at Margot and she is smiling and he says, "This is it."

"I love it," she says.

"It's not much, really. But it's mine."

"It's wonderful."

They stand there for a moment, on the grassy top of the cliff, the house below them, and they can see out to the peninsula that cuts the lake in half, the silvery birch trees that grow on it. The afternoon is hot and humid and Henry knows from looking at the weather that they may get thunderstorms later, and he secretly hopes so, the drama of it all, the windswept water and the rain falling in torrents while he and Margot sit on the screened-in porch and drink wine and watch the lightning expose the sky.

"Let's unload," Henry says.

And so down the steps they go, with Margot carrying their two bags while Henry manages a cooler and two bags of groceries on top of it. He shopped the night before at Safeway for everything they might need, not wanting to have to leave here for anything.

And then they are inside the musty cabin, the door opening onto his simple bedroom with its double bed, and then down the stairs into the one room that contains the kitchen and a small living area framed by a big stone fireplace.

Henry runs around opening everything, aware of how stale it all smells, and then he opens a bottle of white wine and they move out onto the deck that sits right above the lake. He raises the umbrella on the outdoor table and they sit down now and he pours them both glasses of the wine and hands one across to Margot.

"This is so lovely," she says.

"It's hot," he says.

"I love it."

"Cheers," says Henry.

"Cheers."

"So I didn't ask," Henry says. "But where did you say you were going?"

"Canyon Ranch."

"What?"

"It's a retreat center in western Massachusetts. I have gone there before. Do yoga and clear my head. Eat healthy. I told Chad I just needed a break."

"Well, I can't promise you that we will eat superhealthy. But we should go swimming. The water is beautiful."

"It looks cold."

"Refreshing. It's really lovely."

Margot sips her wine. "I feel like I am on a first date. I can't imagine you seeing me in a bathing suit right now."

Henry smiles and waves his hand outward. There are other houses across the way, but there is no sign of another person anywhere. "We don't need bathing suits," he says. "We have the lake to ourselves."

Margot laughs. "No way."

Henry raises his glass. "Maybe if I get you drunk first."

"You're bad," Margot says. "Henry Gold, what has happened to you?"

"Just making up for lost time," he says, and as soon as he does, he regrets it, for it shatters the simplicity of the moment and brings the past roaring into the present.

Margot stands up then and walks over to the railing of the deck and looks down to the water, toward his dock, which juts out into the lake.

"How about a canoe ride instead?" she says.

"You got it."

And Henry appreciates her grace, her ability to move them both back to here, and in the canoe they move slowly out in the lake, the water like glass as the narrow green boat slices through it. Henry is in the back with the paddle and Margot faces him, and soon they are out past the peninsula that defines the cove and into the broader expanse of the lake.

"Oh, look," Margot says.

Henry follows her eyes to the resident pair of loons floating some twenty yards away from them. Henry, with one long pull on the paddle, steers the boat in their direction. He loves this feeling, the effortless glide, and he loves even more the look of joy on Margot's face as they come within five yards of the large black-and-white birds, who then, one following the other, dive under the water, visible for a moment as sleek shadows before they disappear into the depths together.

Margot, 2012

She wants to love all of this, his small cabin, the deep mountain lake with the clear water where you can see the bottom even when it's deep, the forest that goes right to the shoreline, the high she is getting from the wine, but most of all, the two of them, how easy they are together, and this part, in particular, astonishes her. How can they be so comfortable with each other when by all rights they should be complete strangers?

Margot wants to love all of it, but part of her feels claustrophobic, even in all this open air, maybe nothing more than a nagging sense of self-doubt, or as simple as the idea that he drove her here, leaving her car in the Stamford parking lot, and isn't that such an obvious place for it to be?

They ride the entire lake in his canoe. Back at the cabin, they pour new glasses of wine and, together in the small kitchen, prep dinner, moving around each other with ease, her bending simply to his lead as he asks her if she can make the salad while he marinates the steaks. Outside, the thunder-clouds have started to move in, and Margot can see them thick and heavy and dark above the hills on the other shore, while above them a bright sun still beams down.

Henry looks nervously at the sky. "I want to get these on the grill before it comes," he says. "I never cook inside here if I can help it."

The first crack of thunder hits just as they sit down at the picnic table inside the screened-in porch. Margot jumps a little.

"That make you nervous?" Henry asks.

"A little," she says. "I'm not used to being out here."

Henry laughs and they both look out at the lake, where the wind has picked up suddenly. Margot can see the trees on the peninsula bending under its weight and then she hears the rain before she sees it, like the sound of an oncoming train, and they both turn at the same time and watch it move across the water until it reaches them, pounding on the roof, some of the spray coming through the screen to where they sit.

"Holy shit," Henry says. "Now this is a storm."

"Should we go in?" Margot asks.

"Never," says Henry, and as he says it, lightning strikes somewhere out near the point, just across the lake from them, a blur of light in the gathering darkness, followed instantly by an earthshaking crack, and Margot says, "You sure?"

"Positive," Henry says. "Listen: You know what I love about this?"

"What?"

"The cruelest thing in the world is the march of time. It just keeps going and I know we can't ever stop it. Except on days like this and in a place like this—do you know what I mean? You can slow it down if you try and maybe it's just an illusion, but illusions are real in their own way. This afternoon, for me, felt almost like an entire lifetime. Like that canoe ride could have been a year long, in a good way. Does that make sense?"

"I love your mind," Margot says.

And they eat then and the steak is good and tender and the salad crisp and there is a good baguette to bring it all together and around them the rain falls in sheets and the wind rattles the old cabin and bends the trees, but Margot doesn't care, because suddenly she feels like she is home and maybe there is nothing to be afraid of, after all, and it has been a long time since she has really felt that way.

After dinner, they stand in the screened-in porch, staring out at the storm over the cove, and Henry puts his arm around her and she leans into him. The wind is moving the water on the small lake in great sideways waves that splash over his dock below. They stand there for a while in silence, and maybe Henry is right, that you can slow time if you just try really hard, if you give in to silence and give in to storms like this. She has lived forty-two years and for the first time she is realizing how profoundly beautiful something as simple as a thunderstorm can be.

Soon, though, the wind dies down and the sky starts to lighten and the only thunder they hear is far off in the distance. From the north side of the lake, the sun emerges through the clouds and they watch its golden light spread to where they stand and they can see the fast-moving clouds disappearing above the hills that surround them until, other than the water that is still running everywhere and the steam suddenly burning off the deck, it is as if the storm never visited here.

That night, the moon is stuck behind the hill across from them and they can see it not yet risen and gauzy through the trees. The stars are out in force and the bright stripe of the Milky Way looks close enough to touch above them. It is warm.

"It's dark enough now," Margot says.

"What do you mean?"

"To swim. I want to swim now. You won't be able to see me."

"Don't be so sure," Henry says.

Margot takes off then, through the screened-in porch and out onto the lawn and down toward the dock. She can hear Henry behind her, following. When she reaches the dock, she doesn't hesitate, quickly peeling off her T-shirt and unfastening her bra and then wriggling out of her jeans and sliding her underwear down. He is next to her now and she can hear him doing the same thing, but she doesn't look over, because she wants to be the first one in the water.

And then she is running the four or five steps to the end of the dock and letting herself go like a child, jumping as far as she can, and then hitting the water with that surprise, and she is under. She comes up and pushes her hair out of her face just in time to see Henry's nude body launching off the dock toward her.

"Oh, it's cold," she says when he pops up next to her.

"Are you kidding?" Henry says, and then shouts, "It's beautiful!"

And his voice echoes off the hills and back to them.

Margot swims in then toward the dock until her feet reach the bottom near the side of it. Henry is with her. She is with him. He is in front of her, and in the dark, with the water up to their shoulder, he leans his face into hers and they kiss, softly at first, and then with urgency.

"I'm an ice cube," Margot says.

"It feels good," Henry says.

"Let's go in."

Then in the dark they are gathering their clothes into their hands and running up the small incline to the screened-in porch, and then they are inside and wrapping themselves in towels, and Margot is aware of his eyes on her in that moment when she came into the light of the kitchen, dripping wet and nude, and she does not care. Henry is behind her, his arms around her, his mouth on her neck, and she is lifting her head to allow him to kiss her on the nape, and she reaches her hand behind her and deftly drops his towel, and he is in her hand now, full and familiar.

It is fast and furious. Her hands splayed out on the wooden kitchen table, Henry behind her, that moment when he enters her, the feel of him, his hands strongly on her hips, his breath in her ear, and she is loud, for no one can hear them.

Afterward, he collapses on her back and his arms are slumped around her, his warm face pressed against the back side of her heart. They stand there for a while like that, apart but together, curved like a sculpture.

Henry, 2012

Sometime after midnight, Henry builds a fire, and it takes a while for it draw, since it is not that cold outside, but the kindling is dry, and soon they are sitting cross-legged in front of it, still wrapped in towels, watching and listening to the flames rise up the chimney. He is mildly and pleasantly drunk. Once he got the fire lit, Henry turned off all the other lights in the house, so it is just the light from the fire, yellow fingers of light licking up the walls.

Margot slides over and puts her head in Henry's lap. He runs his fingers through her hair and says, "I have something to tell you."

"Not tonight," she says. "Don't tell me anything tonight."

"Okay," he says. "Tomorrow, then."

"Tomorrow," she replies sleepily.

Henry stares at the fire and plays with her hair, letting his fingernails graze across her scalp, and the last thing she says before he hears her softly snoring is "Oh, that feels good."

For a while he stays like that, listening to her snore, watching the dance of the flames, and then he slowly tries to wake her and she comes to just enough for him to help her up the stairs and into his bed, her towel opening as he lays her down, the entirety of her visible to him for a moment, and then he brings the sheets and the blanket up over her and she moans pleasantly and turns over on her side.

Back downstairs, Henry does not want to sleep. He has this manic electric energy he used to associate with late-night sessions of writing, when the words seemed to come to him from somewhere else and he was just a repository for them, though he never told anyone that, for it always sounded pretentious to him and he wasn't quite sure he believed it himself.

He walks outside onto the deck. The fire in the fireplace was totally for effect, for it is still midsummer-hot out on the mountain lake, and as he walks toward the railing, his towel falls, but he doesn't care.

God, he loves this place. There are houses on the other side of the lake, but they are all darkened, as they often are, other than the big weekends like the Fourth of July.

But every time he comes here, it is as if something goes out of him; all the petty concerns and work and the things that pick at him—big and small, from his inability to write anymore to the idea that he married the wrong woman—disappear as quickly as the sun vanishes over the hills.

Now, standing against the waist-high railing, Henry looks out at the black water stretching over to the peninsula, the trees on that narrow spit of land rising up darkly in contrast to the lighter sky. In the distance then, and all of sudden, he hears the coyotes, like the shrill cries of children on a playground, voices more ancient than Keats, rising higher and higher in an endless gyre.

Margot, 2012

The sun wakes her. Or it is the unmistakable smell of breakfast—coffee, bacon, and eggs—moving upstairs to where she lies?

Margot rolls onto her back. She runs her hand through her hair and considers the room. It is small and wood-paneled and musty and warm now from the sun pouring in through the shadeless window. There is not much to it. An old bureau with a mirror above it is the only furnishing other than the simple wood-framed double bed.

She is naked. Her bag, unzipped from when she carried it up the stairs yesterday afternoon, sits in a corner. The previous evening comes to her then, the wine and the food and the storm, but mostly the frantic sex before she fell asleep in front of the fire. She has a vague memory of Henry leading her upstairs. She has an even more vague memory of him climbing into bed with her what seemed only a few hours ago, turning for a moment and seeing the misty dawn rise off the lake out the window behind her head before curling into him and falling back asleep. And now she is not sure she wants to leave this warmth. There is something pleasing about not moving, she thinks, for when you don't move, there is no possibility you can ruin everything.

Margot reluctantly rises and dresses in shorts and slips a T-shirt over her head and makes her way downstairs. The room smells equally of bacon and woodsmoke. The big windows look out to the lake and a sunny day and the sliding glass door to the deck is open.

"Hey, you're up," Henry says, turning from the stove to look over his shoulder when she reaches the bottom step and enters the room.

"Barely," Margot says, and she goes to him, wraps her arms around him where he stands scrambling eggs. "I would kiss you, but I am afraid my breath would melt a dragon."

"I wouldn't care," Henry says.

"I would," she says.

"You missed the coyotes."

"Coyotes?"

"They were out last night. Magnificent. Everywhere."

"Don't tell me. I won't go outside again."

Henry laughs. "They're more afraid of us. Don't worry."

"Don't be so sure."

They eat breakfast at the outdoor table on the deck, the umbrella shielding them from the bright morning sun. There is a light wind and the sunlight plays off the water, and when

Margot looks down the narrow expanse of lake from here, it is like thousands of tiny pieces of glass reflecting back at them.

Margot takes out her phone and it occurs to her that she has not looked at it once since she has been here. This must be a first, not being permanently tethered to it, and then she also realizes she doesn't have a signal, and a slight feeling of panic comes over her and pulls her back to the rest of her life. What if Chad has been trying to reach her? Alex or Emma? Anyone?

"I need to call home," she says.

"There's a phone inside," Henry says.

"No, I can't use that. I'm supposed to be in Massachusetts. I won't be able to explain the caller ID."

"Of course," says Henry. "I don't know what I was thinking. I guess I forgot we were being illicit."

After breakfast, they go for a walk, the way they came in, up his narrow dirt road to the other dirt road. There is a hillside Henry knows about where you can get a cell signal. It is not far, he tells her, though they walk what feels like two miles, past old farmhouses tucked up tight on the sides of the road, unleashed dogs running up and barking at them as they walk. They go by another, smaller lake, this one without houses, a wall of evergreens coming up to the shoreline on all sides except for the road that runs past it. Then they are climbing a road that is little more than a driveway, parts of it washed out from the rainfall last night, and at the top of it they find themselves in a broad, high meadow, with waist-high grass as far as the eye can see.

"Check now," Henry says.

Margot removes her phone from her pocket.

"Two bars," she says.

She has three texts. All of them are from Chad last night. The first one says, "How are u? Having fun?" The other two are simply question marks, as she didn't answer the first.

For a moment, the guilt gathers over her like a small storm and she thinks of her husband in his office right now, looking down through the canyons of buildings, and for all her doubts about what he does with his time, in truth she has no evidence that he has ever strayed from her, and here she is, four hundred miles to the north in a field with another man, still able to feel him inside her from the night before.

Margot types back. "Sorry. Battery died and fell asleep early last night. All well." The amazing ease of texting, she thinks. She could be anywhere.

Margot looks up from this intrusion and sees Henry smiling at her.

"Come here," he says.

Margot walks to him and he opens his arms and she moves into them. He brings her tight to him and she buries her face in his chest.

"There's something I have to tell you," Henry says from above her.

Margot shakes her head in his chest. "I don't want to know."

Henry says, "They made me write that letter."

Margot steps back from him. "Which letter?"

"The one I sent you on the Vineyard. After what happened

at the winery. A guy who worked for your father came to see me. I don't remember his name. Tall guy with a British accent. He sat in my parents' kitchen."

"Kiernan."

"Yes. That was his name. I felt like I didn't have a choice. They said if I wrote it, they would drop the charges and I would be allowed to finish school."

Margot shook her head. "You didn't have a choice. It was so long ago. Please, let it go."

"I know. But I have carried it with me all these years. What if I'd said no? There is no greater act of cowardice as a poet than a failure to tell the truth."

"You were a kid, Henry. They would have ruined your life."

"It felt ruined anyway. Until that moment I saw you standing across from the Shake Shack. How I felt then reminded me that I had been asleep for a long time, you know? Just going through the motions. I keep asking myself, Is this real? You know what I mean?"

Margot nods. "Can we go back? I want to swim. I don't want to think anymore. I just want to swim."

And on the walk back to his cabin, down the long stretch of dirt road, Margot hates the conversation they just had, not just for what he said, which doesn't surprise her, but for how she handled it. That she managed in that moment to be strategic in her response, as if he were someone she was having a debate with, someone on one of her boards, and not the man she had opened herself to more than any other. Worse still is why she did it. As if by downplaying how Henry responded to the box her father put Henry in, as he had put so many others in over time, could somehow erase the big weight she has never unburdened herself of and that she knows she cannot go one more night carrying alone.

Henry is the first one in the water. She admires him as she walks down the small hill to the dock, admires his long torso as he hurls himself in a smooth dive off the end of it, curving up in the air before slicing cleanly into the lake, so clear that she can see him underneath it, a long silvery shape, moving out deep into the cove before surfacing.

"Come in," Henry says, on his back now, his head out of the water, improbably halfway to the peninsula. "It's great."

Margot stands there for a moment, considering the water, feeling slightly silly in her bikini, then remembering he has seen far more of her than this, and that the thing about water is that it doesn't get any warmer by staring at it.

"Do it," Henry shouts.

And she lets herself go then, and there is the feeling of being in the air, of her feet leaving the strafed wood of the dock, rising up in an arc, and then the clear, cool water taking her breath away as she plummets underneath it, propelling herself forward with long strokes toward Henry.

Margot waits until dark. She waits until after dinner. She waits until the two gin and tonics have erased her doubt.

They are out on the deck. Henry grilled salmon and corn

for dinner and afterward they did the dishes together, washing them by hand in the small sink, drying them and putting them away, moving around each other with the ease of the long-married couple they should have been. At one point, Henry turned to her and she proffered her face to him and he leaned down and kissed her and looked at her with his dark eyes, gazing right through her and saying, "Holy shit, I love you."

"I love you, too," she said, and in saying it, she hoped it would be enough to carry them through.

Now, as they sit on the bench next to the railing over the lake, all traces of the sun are gone and the moon is caught in the trees on the opposite shore, not yet risen. The stars are not out yet and the sky is a brilliant sweep of blue. The woods around them breathe with night sounds.

"Henry," Margot says.

"Yes?"

"There is something I have to say."

From a foot away, he shifts his position, sensing something in her voice, and leans in toward her. Margot is grateful for the dark, so that he cannot fully see her face. She is worried she is going to cry and then she is crying, the sobs coming fast, and she cannot stop them.

"Honey, what is it?"

"I can't," Margot says.

"I don't understand."

"Oh, Henry," she says. "I don't know how to say this."

"It's okay. I can handle anything. Really."

Margot stands up then. She walks away from him in the dark. She paces a few feet away and then turns back toward where Henry sits looking up at her expectantly.

"My children have been my life, you know? Alex and Emma. For so long they defined me. They were who I was. They gave me a purpose. And now they are both out of the house and it's different. And I am a terrible person."

"You're being hard on yourself."

"No, I'm not. I'm not being clear, I know. This is so hard."

"I don't understand," Henry says.

"Alex, Alex will turn twenty-one next spring. Do you understand?"

"I'm confused. What do you mean?"

"That night before . . . the night before my father was there. That night in the vineyard?"

"Yes?"

"We made a child that night."

"What do you mean?"

"Alex is your son, Henry."

The silence comes then, and Margot can hear Henry breathing in the pregnant dark across from her and she can hear the timid slap of the lake against the dock below them, the wake from a small boat whose running lights they can see far over on the other side, moving back and forth, trolling for trout.

Henry is on his feet. Please say something, Margot thinks. Say something. Anything.

Margot watches as he walks away from her toward the far

railing and then comes back. She can feel his intensity coming off him in waves. She needs him to speak.

"Say something," she says. "Please."

Henry's voice cracks as he says, "You're kidding, right? Tell me you're fucking kidding. Please tell me you're fucking kidding."

"No," Margot says softly. "I'm sorry."

There is nothing else for her to say, and she realizes that since she has let this out into the world, it is all on his terms, and his time, as it should be. She listens to him pace back and forth. She knows he is gathering his words now like the clouds gathered over the hills earlier and that when they come, they will be forceful. She braces herself.

When Henry finally speaks, his voice surprises her. It is soft and distant at first and he says, "When my father died."

"Yes."

"Well, before he died. When he was dying. I visited him in hospice. My father was a very quiet man. He barely spoke. He almost never expressed emotion. But he was a good man. And the way you knew that was never from anything he said, but from how he lived. How much he loved my mother. How hard he worked. It's funny that I became a poet when the father in my life avoided words. But when I visited him in hospice, he was honest with me in a way that only the dying can be. I asked him . . . I asked him . . . oh, shit," says Henry, and he starts to cry.

Margot stands and Henry says now, his voice rising, "No, sit. Please. I am sorry. But sit."

Margot sits down.

Henry steadies his voice. "When he was dying, I asked him, I asked him if he had any regrets. I expected him to say no. He was not someone who ever complained. About anything. But you know what he said?"

"No," Margot says.

"He said he wished he had a grandson. And the reason he wished this," Henry says, talking fully through tears now, "was not because he didn't love his granddaughter, which he did, for like me, she was his everything. The only time I ever really saw him light up was when Jess came in the room. He was a different person around her. But my father wished he had a grandson because he was old-school, my father, and in the Jewish tradition, sons are very important. They provide the continuity between generations. And looking at my father in bed, the tubes in his arms, the machine beeping every time his oxygen dipped, like some clock counting down the moments to his death, I felt this incredible sadness and an almost paralyzing guilt. I saw all my own failings. Could I have done things differently with Ruth? Where did we come apart? My God, we had a beautiful child and Ruth had always wanted another one, but I had this nagging doubt, and maybe it's because I knew my marriage would fail. That it would be my fault. But what if I had worked harder? Done more? Found a way to be present? Maybe we would have stayed together. Maybe we would have had another child. Maybe we would have had a son. And my proud father, selfless to the very end, the best goddamn man I have ever known, a man I will never be, would have gone to the other side without a single regret."

"I see," Margot says.

"I'm not looking for affirmation," says Henry.

"I don't know what to say."

"Don't say anything," Henry says. "You just need to know what you stole from me."

These last words cut her, the sharp diamond edge of truth, and they are cruel only in their honesty, and she knows this, but it is as if his knife just punctured her lungs in a search of her heart, and now she is struggling to breathe.

"I'm sorry," Margot says.

"How?" Henry says, raising his voice to a shout through his tears. "How could you do this to me?"

"I don't know," Margot whispers. "I don't know."

"Oh, God," Henry says, spinning away from her. He moves to the railing and leans over it. Margot listens to him crying now, the sobs catching in his throat, gagging like he might vomit, and she wants more than ever to go to him, but she knows she cannot.

Henry, 2012

They drive in silence. They are as separate as two people can be in the front seat of a small car. Henry grips the wheel with both hands and stares straight ahead at the road disappearing under the tires, and Margot is leaning against the passenger-side door, her head wedged into the small space between the door and her seat. The only sounds come from outside the car, the swish of the windshield wipers as they displace the light rain that started that morning.

The previous night is a dream. Henry is exhausted. He remembers crying until he couldn't cry anymore. He remembers a fractured dawn coming to the lake, the two of them still outside, the sun not yet risen behind the hills, while above the water a dense mist rose up into the air.

"I didn't know," Margot had said, and then: "I knew, but I pretended I didn't know. I wanted him to be Chad's just because it was so much easier. And I thought if I believed that, it would be true. But then every time I looked at my son, it was you I saw."

"Does Chad know?" Henry asked.

Margot shook her head.

"How could he not?"

"People see what they want to see."

"And Alex has no idea."

"No," said Margot.

"Dear God," Henry said.

Now, driving down Interstate 91 in the rain, Henry is haunted by the photo she showed him on her phone: Alex, tall, slender, standing on a Manhattan street, wearing a coat and tie. The effect of seeing him shakes Henry, for Alex is a perfect amalgam of the two of them, her coloring except for the eyes, which might as well have been lifted off his own face and handed to this child of his he has been robbed of knowing.

There is no need for him to take a test. You know your child when you see him, even if, seeing him for the first time, he is standing on the cusp of manhood.

Henry looks over at Margot. Her eyes are closed, her head kicked back, though he can tell she is not sleeping. Is there anything more lovely than a beautiful woman in repose? And thinking this, Henry wonders what kind of fool he must be to succumb to a love that is harsher than the darkest vicissitudes of life itself. Perhaps there is some inherent flaw in him that he has ignored all these years, moving through life stuck in his head and never fully assessing things. Is that possible?

When does it end? Maybe the whole thing—the depth of his love, his obsession, the way she made him feel before last night in the dark—is all some grand illusion, a big fucking lie that he has been way too gullible to recognize, the ancient cliché of the blind poet who can see in his mind great horizons but misses anything right in front of him. What a terrible fool you are, Henry Gold.

As if feeling the heat of his eyes on her, Margot opens hers. Henry looks back to the road.

"I'm going to leave Chad," she says.

"I can't think about that," Henry says.

"I'm not doing it for you. I'm doing it for myself. I know you think I am a shitty, horrible person, and you are right, I am. But I need to start living for once. For myself."

If this is an invitation for him to correct her, Henry is not yet willing to do that. Instead, he just nods and looks back ahead. "Okay," he says.

The rain picks up then and Henry focuses on the road. As they are coming through Massachusetts, the rain falls hard and they don't talk anymore. It is as if everything they could possibly say has been said for now, though how could that be true?

For the first time in a long time, Henry can't wait to be alone.

Margot, 2012

She tells Chad at Artisanal, a busy bistro just off Madison. She chooses the restaurant deliberately, as it is one of his places downtown, which he considers his domain, and the type of noisy venue where he likes to take a group of clients who will eat perfectly executed steak frites while Chad keeps the thousand-dollar bottles of Pomerol flowing and orders rare cheeses from the restaurant's own *fromagerie* cave for the table.

It has been three days since Henry dropped her off at the park and ride in Stamford and helped her retrieve her bags and then turned his back on her. She has texted him three times and left him a voice mail and he hasn't respond to any of them. This makes Margot afraid, but she made a commitment to herself that night at the lake to live honestly from now on, regardless of the consequences.

And so it is with steely purpose that as soon as the drinks come, she tells Chad everything. She braces herself when she begins, saying, “I need a divorce.” The words are chosen as carefully as the restaurant. She doesn’t say “I want a divorce,” but that she needs one. Then slowly and methodically, she tells him the entire story.

Chad knows about Henry, of course—the young Henry, that is—but not that he has stumbled back into her life. While she talks, telling him about the chance meeting at Columbus Circle, her seeking him out later, the dinner at Marea, the trip to Vermont, Chad looks at her blankly, though she can see his mind racing, his hand now and again running through his thin hair, a tic he has when he is stressed.

What kind of man, Margot thinks, listens to his wife telling him about her love for another man, telling him that she had sex with him at a small lake cabin in the Vermont mountains, and acts no different than he would have if he had been summoned upstairs to be told he was being relieved of his job?

It is a test of sorts. She almost wishes he would strike her. A flash of anger he cannot control and feels terrible about afterward, out of character but understandable, given what he has learned.

“It’s the right thing for both of us,” Margot says. “I don’t believe you love me anymore, either.”

Chad cracks a thin smile. “I don’t even know what love is at our age,” he says.

“It’s no different than it ever was,” says Margot.

“I’m not so sure about that,” Chad says.

“You have had affairs, yes?”

Chad shakes his head. "No. Never."

"I'm shocked. I always assumed. All those nights you stayed over in the city. Your trips. I thought I was just being French about it all," she says, though she doesn't really mean this, either, and as soon as she says it, she realizes that candor will take practice, that it's one thing to do it on the large scale, but a lifetime of cultivation that values small lies and half-truths will be hard to overcome.

"I haven't," he says. "I always knew there was an imbalance between us, you see? I always loved you more than you loved me. That was clear to me. I wasn't your first choice and I knew that."

"Why did you marry me, then?"

"Because you were pregnant. I thought it was mine."

This takes Margot's breath away. "You know? About Alex?"

Chad sits back in his chair, takes a long pull off his martini. "Of course. I'm not stupid, Margot. I didn't know right away. But after a while, it was pretty clear to me."

"Why didn't you ever say anything? All these years?"

Chad shrugged. "What could I say?"

"I don't deserve you," Margot says.

"You're right," Chad says. "You don't."

Henry, 2012

It is all a dream, a crazy, foggy dream, and in the dream there are words, and before there are words, there are letters, and he has never really considered letters before, just small things, right, like the invisible grains of sand that make up glass? And simply foundational, just as a brick is just a brick until you put some together, and then you have a wall, and why hasn't he ever thought about them before in quite this way? Each one is as different as a snowflake, and why are there only twenty-six of them?

And the words themselves aren't really words anymore, but just naked sounds and raw aboriginal music, and when he strings them together, they sound like songs, amazing and old, songs that were there before language was there. They are songs that were there before he was here. Before anyone he loves was ever here. Are they about him? Can they be about him? Does it matter? Where does he end and art begin?

It is hot in his apartment. The air is close. The air is stifling. Henry doesn't care.

He writes with a pen on paper, wearing only his underwear, and the sweat comes off his forehead and as soon as he finishes writing, he moves over to his laptop on the small desk and takes the words and types them in as fast as he can, and he likes this, seeing them appear on the screen in front of him, as if they are fully formed and about to be.

He drinks. He stares at them. He puts a jazz record on the stereo and plays it as loudly as he can. He stares at the words. He changes them. He changes them back. He thinks of new words. He builds sand castles on the page. He tears them down. He builds them again, and this time more ornately. He hates the writing. He loves what he has written. He hates what he has written. It is a cycle that exists without day or night, until he is so exhausted that he tries to sleep, and when he cannot sleep, he ventures out into the city and walks and walks until it hurts to walk anymore and all he can do is lie on his unkempt bed and stare at a ceiling blanker than the page.

Henry is up all night. There is a delicious insanity to it, to watching the dawn appear like gold to the east and then slowly cast its lazy blanket over the city to where he stares out the window to the Hudson and to the first tendrils that rake the the fat blueness stretching toward the rising Palisades on the opposite shore.

Then he is dressing, a suit, for some reason, wrinkled and well overdue for the dry cleaner's, and for a while he considers shoes and then chooses, oddly, a pair of sandals, but it doesn't matter. Then he is out into the city, and Henry has no sense of time, but he knows from the light that it is early.

Henry moves across the city in an odd diagonal, meandering like a child who doesn't want to get home too quickly from school. He walks initially through the park and then drifts down Fifth, and it is all marvel, the race everyone appears to be in to get somewhere, while for him the day in front is as long as the summer itself.

He walks for more than hour. And then, in front of him, at the split of Fifth and Broadway, is the object of his desire, the great prow of a ship jutting out into the sea of Manhattan, the Flatiron Building.

He moves down Fifth toward the main entrance. People stream in and out. Henry goes to a lamppost across from the glass doors and casually leans against it. He will stay here as long as he needs to.

Henry's focus is singular. Discipline has always guided him. Discipline made him a shortstop once and discipline later made him into a poet. The passion came from his mother and the work ethic from his father. And now what he needs is patience.

The people go in and out all morning. Henry has little sense of time. How long has he been standing here?

And then, lunch, or what must be lunch, for suddenly the doors are busier, people of all kinds streaming out onto the street, dissipating in different directions, on their phones, looking at watches, moving with clutched briefcases. And then just as suddenly, he is there, Alex, fast as smoke, coat and tie on, chinos, and Henry knows him instantly, would know him anywhere, and next to him is a young blond woman in a suit and they are laughing as they move out of the building and head north, passing only a few feet in front of Henry, and he sees, for the first time, his son in profile, and it is like falling backward through time to his own slender youth.

For a moment, he considers following the two of them. But a small gesture stops him. Alex reaches his arm out suddenly and stretches it around the woman's back, bringing her close to him for a moment, and she turns her head up to his and smiles, and they are both so endlessly young and pretty, it breaks his heart to see it, and they are laughing again now, moving into each other, and Henry thinks they deserve to be as alone as they believe they are, the city colliding all around them.

Margot, 2012

The following day, Margot pays a visit to her parents' Central Park West penthouse. She calls her mother to tell her she is coming, that she has news, but she doesn't say anything else. Her mother pries, but Margot says, "I will be there in an hour. I need to talk to you and Dad."

Her mother meets her at the door and they move out to the patio, where her father sits in a cast-iron chair painted white at a table with a diet soft drink on it, still saluting the brand he managed for thirty years. Her father pivots his head away from the view and toward her, the park far below them, the buildings of the Upper East Side rising up over beyond it, and for a moment Margot's eyes go to a tall, thin building, and she remembers that they call this building "Donald Trump's penis," since it was the first high rise he built in New York.

A minor stroke two years ago has left her father's face

slightly off center and has affected his gait when he walks, but otherwise, he looks well for his eighties, a full head of hair, and those clear, sharp wolf eyes.

"Margot," he practically barks at her. "Sit down."

Margot slides a chair out from the table, hearing the soft scrape of it across the tiled balcony, and her mother sits down across from her.

"Hi, Daddy," she says.

"View never gets old, does it?" her father says.

"No," Margot replies with a thin smile.

"What can I help you with?" her father says.

"Nothing, actually."

"Oh, your mother said you needed to talk."

"I do, but I don't need any help."

Her father reaches out with his big hand and grabs the can of soda, takes a long pull of it. The habit he picked up decades ago—six to ten cans of it a day—he is still continuing. All that caffeine, Margot thinks.

"What is it, then?"

"I have asked Chad for a divorce," Margot says.

Her mother gasps slightly and says, "Oh, sweetie, why?"

Her father sits up straighter in his chair and looks at her. "Fullers don't get divorced," he says.

"Well, this one does," says Margot.

"He's having an affair, isn't he?" her dad says. "That bastard."

"No," Margot says. "I am. Not that it matters. That's not why. I am not in love with him. And I never was."

"Oh, for Christ's sake, Margot," her mother says. "You aren't a teenager anymore."

"I know. I am not asking your permission. I wanted you to know."

"Say you're sorry and get on with it," her father says.

"No, I won't do that. I am doing this for myself."

"You're going to need a good lawyer. Chad will take you to the cleaner's. Karen, get the phone and get me Doug Brenniman."

"No," Margot says firmly. "I don't need your help."

"Yes, you goddamn do," her father says.

"No, I don't. And now I am leaving. I have a busy day."

Margot stands and her father looks up at her and says, "Sit back down."

"No," she says. "I have to go."

"Wait," her father says.

"Good-bye, Daddy," Margot says. "Bye, Mom."

And with that she is back through the expansive apartment to the elevator, moving down to the street and to the new day.

It is all very civil. They get lawyers by the end of the week. The lawyers talk and they don't. Chad moves into the guest room, and in the mornings he is gone before she wakes. The following week, they will go to Maine and speak with Emma. And then they will talk to Alex in the city. The money is primarily Margot's, the expansive trust fund she brought into the marriage. She quickly agrees that Chad is entitled to a generous annuity. She doesn't want the fucking money. She doesn't care about the fucking money. This is his major concern, but now he won't have to worry about any of it. He can get his apartment in TriBeCa. Once that is settled, there is little else to talk about. The kids are old enough. There are no custody questions.

Margot sleeps late and then she forces herself to make coffee. She is not hungry ever, it seems, and often doesn't eat until dinner. She can feel herself losing weight and knows she looks like shit. But she is not depressed—no, something else is happening to her. It is something not so easy to grasp.

There is a heavily wooded park near their house, and in the mornings she goes there after her coffee and just walks. She walks up and over the small hills and through the leafy pathways, and she likes the way the sunlight is obscured and dappled at her feet and she likes the sounds of the birds, and now and again she sees joggers or young women pushing strollers as she once did herself, but mostly it is just her and her thoughts, and this is how it should be now.

Margot walks until her legs ache and then she returns home and paints. She paints with something approaching fury, her hand dancing over the canvas, the brushstrokes coming easily to her, as if it is not her hand and her mind guiding them, but something else. She doesn't know if it is any good and she doesn't care. She just loves the blank physicality of it, of taking the white space and filling it with color and shape and form until it is something that not even she understands.

She paints until she feels the siren song of the bottle of chilled white wine in the fridge, the glass or two in the late afternoon, which feels both like a complete indulgence and a necessity, for it is then that she finally begins to let go and makes her daily call to Henry, hoping that for once it will not go unanswered. Her calls are bordering on harassment now, since she has not talked to him since the drive home from Vermont. It has been two weeks.

Her heart sinks as once again it goes directly to voice mail.

The following morning, she wakes to driving rain, so instead of taking her walk, she finds herself in the small downtown and then in the independent bookstore on the main street. She has a vague idea of wanting something new to read, a rainy-day book to make her forget what she cannot stop thinking about, which is Henry, whom she is suddenly worried about—what if he stepped off a curb and got struck by speeding taxi and is in a hospital, or, worse, dead? Would anyone have any reason to reach out and tell her?

And while thinking this, Margot finds herself browsing the magazine rack and her eye is drawn to a copy of *Art in New England.*

Margot opens it and is leafing through when a full-page ad catches her eye. The image is of a woman painting in front of an easel, but the words say "The National Association of Schools of Art and Design is pleased to offer portfolio day,

August 4, New York University, New York City. Meet with over thirty graduates of fine arts programs."

That afternoon she returns home, and with a driving rain smashing against the windows, she lines up all the paintings she has done over the past two years against the white wall in her dining room.

Oh God, Margot thinks, looking them over, they all suck, don't they? Then she remembers something Henry used to say about not self-editing and that the real courage lies in taking what you have created and spinning it out into the world, letting it speak for itself and knowing that no matter how good you think it is, some will hate it even if others love it. And that none of that matters, when you get right down to it, for you have to learn to separate yourself from the work, even if your soon-to-be ex-husband thinks you are painting vaginas, which you are certainly not.

Margot gets her camera. Methodically she takes photos of every one of her paintings. Later, after she receives the prints, she chooses twenty of them, the ones she admires the most, the paintings that she believes speak most to what she is trying to do, which even for her is hard to try to explain. It is almost as if the paintings represent particular emotions she felt at a specific time, and their abstractness contributes to this idea. Margot goes with her gut and then mounts them carefully on black-matted paper, loving this part of it, the labor of the installation.

On a sunny and mild August morning, Margot takes the train into the city. As the train rocks back and forth on the tracks, she sits looking placidly out the window, clutching her carefully crafted portfolio tightly in her hands, as if someone might try to steal it from her. It is late morning and the train is half-empty, most of the commuters having already arrived at Grand Central hours before. Nevertheless, there is a mix of men in suits going into work late and women ten years younger than she with bored children. Across from her is an old woman with a run in her stockings, gripping the metal pole in front of her with her small hands. Margot moves her eyes from the woman's legs up to her face and is startled to see the woman staring back at her, grimacing, as if she is in pain. Margot quickly looks away and wonders if she wears a similar look.

Is she a fool? Oh, maybe she should just get off at Harrison, the next stop, and turn around and go home. But then Margot steels herself. No, she must do this.

Soon she is out in the city and walking with the portfolio under her arm, and it feels good to walk, the sense of purpose. She stops once to check her phone to make sure she has the address right. The event is at NYU, some art auditorium, and it is not lost on her that the university is where Henry works, though she also knows it is a huge place.

As she enters the auditorium, the sea of people threatens to overwhelm her and she suddenly feels dizzy, and it takes all of her focus to move over to the registration table on her left and stand in line. Looking around at the other artists also holding similar portfolios, Margot thinks she has made a huge mistake. They are all half her age at least, and she looks like someone's mother. A boy in front of her with giant tribal hoops exploding through his earlobes turns around to look at her, and on his shoulder is a rat. At first she thinks it must be fake, but then it turns its narrow face toward Margot and she takes a quick step backward, causing people behind her to laugh.

Margot takes a deep breath, and in a moment the line deposits her at the registration table.

"Margot Baldwin," she says, and then corrects herself, remembering that now she is using her maiden name. "Fuller. Margot Fuller."

Soon she is drifting through the crowd to the tables with the big numbers above them, young people all around her moving like sheep through the large, well-lit room. Minutes later, she is sitting across from two men, one bald, with a huge gray beard, and the other slender and clean-shaven, with blocky black glasses.

"Show us what you have," the bearded one says.

Margot opens the portfolio in front of them. She slowly goes through it.

Blocky Glasses says, "It's very interesting what you are doing. All this play. The way you use light. Let me ask you something. You ever think of taking it off the wall?"

Margot feels like she should know what this means, but she doesn't. "I'm sorry?"

"You know, an installation. Greater dimensionality. Perhaps even something time-based. Painting is so . . . well, you know."

"Yes," she says, though she has no idea.

It is at her third critique, this time in front of a woman with long gray hair from a school in Vermont, that she finally feels comfortable.

"Oh, I like what you are doing," the woman says.

"Really?"

"Yes. There is such intentionality here. And confidence. You can just see it in the brushstrokes. Would you describe yourself as methodical? "

Margot nods. "I think so."

"I want to see what you do when you let go," the woman tells her. "The talent is obvious. But the work feels constrained to me. If you were to work with me, I would want you to reach deeper, and I think there is the potential for real power."

An hour later, Margot walks out into bright sunshine. It is indescribable how she feels, like layers of an onion have been peeled away from her and she is both suddenly raw and very much alive. She wants a drink. This has been a triumph in her opinion, a significant one, and she wants to share it with someone.

Henry, she thinks, I need to see Henry. And she stops on the street then and Googles him with her phone, looking for where his office might be, for could he be there? She is already at NYU.

And then she is walking several blocks to Green Street, and the miracle that is the phone tells her exactly where to go, and soon she is right in front of the town house that houses NYU's creative writing program. Inside the doorway, there is a directory, and she sees that his office is on the second floor. The place seems mostly empty, apart from a few voices she can hear somewhere on the first floor, and Margot bounds up the carpeted stairs.

She is in a narrow hallway that curves around to the right and she follows it, and the third door is marked HENRY GOLD. The door is closed and the white erasable board on it contains a note in Henry's handwriting: *I might or might not be back.*

"Are you looking for Henry?" a voice says suddenly, and Margot turns and sees a slender black man with big red glasses on.

"Yes," Margot says.

The man looks her quickly up and down. "Are you a friend?"

"Yes," Margot says, and she doesn't like this question, as if he knows something terrible and is about to tell her. Henry's note has unnerved her, though it could be entirely innocent, couldn't it? The kind of thing Henry would write as a joke?

"Oh," the man says, looking over at the note. "He hasn't come here in weeks. I was thinking of trying Ruth, his ex-wife, later to see if she had heard from him. I was starting to get worried. It's not like him. I mean, he disappears up to Vermont, but he always tells us. Were you supposed to meet him here?"

"No," says Margot. "He wasn't . . . He wasn't expecting me. I hope he's okay."

"I'm sure he is," the man says.

"Okay," Margot says, and then adds, "Thank you."

Back out in the sunshine, Margot is in a panic. She looks up the narrow street for a moment and tries to collect herself. Where is the best place to get a cab uptown? Before she can think, she is running toward Houston Street, and when she reaches a corner, a yellow cab streams by and she raises her hand. And, thank God, he stops.

"Ninety-second and West End," she says. "And hurry. Please."

"West Side Highway?" the man asks.

"Yes," Margot says. "Please."

They go down a maze of side streets, and at one point the car has to stop dead because a truck in front of them is being unloaded and is blocking the entire street. Morbid images enter her mind: Henry all alone. Henry taking a handful of pills and swallowing them with a stiff drink, Henry doing the unthinkable, the poet choosing to leave this world dramatically. She thinks she might be sick.

Then they are moving again, and once they hit the highway, it is wide open at midday and they are speeding, with the Hudson on her left, past the giant aircraft carrier, and she catches glimpses of midtown through the cross streets, and then they are turning onto Ninety-second, and she thrusts a ten and a twenty at the driver when he pulls over, and he says, "Need change?" but Margot is already out the door.

Margot runs up the sidewalk, and right before she reaches Henry's building, she sees a man coming out of it and she says, "Wait," and he stops and looks at her, this middle-aged woman running madly at him.

He is around her age, tall, wearing a suit, his hair full and silver. "You okay?" he asks.

"Can you let me in the building?" Margot says breathlessly. "I'm worried about my friend."

"Who's your friend?"

"Henry Gold."

"I know Henry. The teacher."

"Is he okay?"

"I think so. I don't know. Haven't seen him, to tell you the truth."

"Can you let me in? Please?"

Margot sees the man considering. He has kind eyes. He is looking at her as if trying to assess if she is insane. A moment later, he says, "You can buzz his apartment."

"Please just let me in," Margot says. "I've known Henry a long time."

"All right," the man says.

Margot is through the lobby and into the elevator and then riding it up to the fourteenth floor. The old box creaks as it goes, settling and then moving again, and her stomach sinks as it slowly lurches, until finally it opens and she is down the hallway to his door.

There is a buzzer, but Margot knocks loudly. "Henry," she says, "Henry, open the door; it's Margot."

Margot knocks again, this time frantically. "Henry, please. If you're in the there, let me in in, please."

And then she hears a click and the door opens. Henry stands in front of her. He is a mess, his hair unkempt, jeans and a T-shirt on, barefoot, but more than that, there is the look in his eyes, slightly wild and manic, like he has been sleeping outside.

"Oh, Henry," Margot says. "I was worried. You wouldn't answer. I went to your office and I saw your note and I didn't know . . ."

Henry shrugs. "I've been working."

Henry turns his back to her and drifts back into the small apartment. Margot follows him, shutting the door behind her, and she is hit immediately by the overwhelming smell of Chinese food. The countertop that separates the little galley kitchen from the living room is littered with take-out containers, dozens of them, some stacked on top of each other, others still open. There are clothes on the floor. The lone window, straight ahead and looking west toward the river between buildings, has a visible covering of dust that diffuses the sunlight.

"When's the last time you were outside?" Margot asks.

Henry smiles wanly. "I have no idea. Days? Sorry about the mess. I've been writing."

"I didn't think you would let me in," Margot says.

Henry ignores this. He goes over to the small desk near the window. It is covered with papers. He picks one up off the top and takes it over to where Margot stands, the few feet she has walked since he opened the door. He motions to the brown couch to her left, a coffee table in front of it.

"Sit down," he says. Margot can feel the energy washing off of him.

She does as Henry asks. She sits on the couch. He looms above her and then thrusts the single sheet of paper into her hands. Margot looks up at him.

"Read it," Henry says. "Please."

"Okay."

Margot looks down at the paper.

Native Son, 2012

You come to me fully born
Like something out of mythology
Not a child or the infant you once must have been
Rather like the story Aristophanes told to Plato
A child of the sun, of course
Separated from me at birth
Clutching your mother's rib in your tiny fist
Raising it in the air as a man
And wondering if you will know me when you see me
Broken twins, the two of us
Love palpable and scouring the plains
And the forests
And the cities of dreams
Until that final day
When I look into your unchanging eyes
And see myself.

When Margot looks up, she is weeping. Henry has his back to her, having moved to the window, but then he turns toward her and strides back.

"It's beautiful," she says. "I am so sorry."

"I know."

"It's really beautiful."

"I'm going to have a drink. You want one?"

"What time is it?" Margot asks.

"Does it matter?"

"I guess not."

Henry pads into the kitchen. Margot hears the sound of glasses, ice, the pop of a bottle releasing its suction. A moment later, Henry is back with a glass, which he hands to her.

"Vodka," he says. "Sorry. All I have left."

Henry sits down next to her on the couch. Margot sips the vodka. At least it's cold. For a moment, they don't say anything.

"I saw him, you know," Henry says.

"Who?"

"Alex."

"Wait. What? Where?"

"Don't worry, I didn't say anything to him. I just wanted to see him."

"Where?"

"At the Flatiron. I waited for him to come out. I just needed to see him with my own eyes."

"Oh my God, Henry," Margot says.

Henry shrugs. Margot looks over at him. His eyes are wet and his face looks so drawn, like that of someone who has been through an exhaustive medical procedure.

"I am so sorry," Margot says.

"I know," says Henry.

"What did you think?"

"He's more beautiful than I could ever put into words."

Margot looks away and she starts to cry. She doesn't want to look at Henry now, for the guilt is more than she can bear. She cries. And Henry doesn't say anything else. They sit in silence. Margot looks around the small, sad apartment. The air is close and there is the slightly sweet, slightly acrid smell of all the Chinese food. Then Margot cannot help it: Between the tears, she starts to laugh. At first it's just a giggle and then she is laughing.

"What?" Henry says.

"This place is so fucking gross," she says, laughing. "It's worse than anything in college."

Henry looks around and nods. The look on his face is almost prideful.

"Yes, it is," he says, and now they are both laughing, and suddenly a siren wails outside, the city sound she has never gotten used to, and at once they both look toward the window and then back at each other.

Henry, 2012

His collection comes out in October, his first in more than a dozen years. His editor at Wesleyan University Press rushes it to publication because, after reading it, she thinks it could compete for the major prizes.

"We're going to submit it to everyone, Henry," she says. "It's that important. Pulitzer. Everyone. I can't tell how you excited we all are."

On a cool early fall night, Henry drives north to Middletown, where the English Department at Wesleyan has invited him to do a reading, and the press is throwing him a book party after.

Getting dressed earlier for it, he put on his jeans and his white shirt and threw a tweed blazer over it and then slipped on brown wing tips. He had this moment of awareness looking at himself in the mirror, a shard of memory of him a lifetime ago in his baseball uniform, and thinking, That is how it is now. We all still wear uniforms. Behold, everyone, the academic poet.

An hour later, Henry stands backstage, behind a curtain with two members of the English faculty. On the stage now, a student is reading, a young Indian girl he met briefly before she went onstage. She was selected to read before he does. Unlike his own experience at Bannister many years ago, she was remarkably self-assured when he met her. She seemed pleased to meet him but was far from intimidated or nervous about having to go out first. From here, he can hear the sound of her voice, capable and with perfect, clear diction, though her words come to him in snatches.

"You ready, Henry?" his editor, Suzanne, asks.

"Sure."

Suzanne goes out first and Henry opens the curtain slightly from the side so he can hear her. He hears his name: "Henry Gold." He hears: "Yale Younger Poet. His work has appeared in *The New Yorker*, the *Iowa Review*," and on and on. "He holds the Wilhelm Chair in Poetry at New York University. Please join me in welcoming . . . Henry Gold."

Henry steps out from the curtain. Suzanne leaves the podium and turns toward him and they meet halfway, and with the applause in the background, he gives her a hug before he steps up to the podium with his book in his hand.

The applause stops. The fecundity of the moment confronts him, one he has learned to enjoy. Henry adjusts the microphone.

Audiences are enormously generous and patient, which

is something that takes time to learn. Henry peers out into the crowd. Three hundred or so, stacked on top of one another, moving up and away from him to the back of the room.

His eyes move from row to row and then he sees Margot, eight rows or so back, and next to her, of course, is her son—his son, he should say—a senior now and a English major. Henry is seeing him in person for only the second time, but that does not matter to him at all.

Henry looks right at Alex, at his soft brown eyes, which he can see even from here. Alex's eyes are mirrors; his chin is upturned and he is looking, naturally, at Henry. Everyone is looking at Henry, but the crowd has shrunk to one.

"'Native Son,'" Henry says, and he begins to read.

ACKNOWLEDGMENTS

I began this novel on a hot summer afternoon in 2014, sitting on the deck of a small lake cabin in northern Vermont and watching a pair of loons dive under the clear, cool water. I finished it six months later over lunch at Three Penny Taproom, and in between, I wrote it in all kinds of places. It was the fastest, by far, I have ever completed a novel, and I can say now that I wrote it with a wind at my back because of the support of so many people.

John Cheever once said that writing is not a competitive sport, which is true, but publishing is a team one. My gratitude begins with everyone at Thomas Dunne Books, starting with Tom himself. Every writer should be fortunate enough to have such a champion. I want to thank Pete Wolverton for his insight and support of this book from the beginning. And, of course, my talented, hardworking, and brilliant editor, Anne

Brewer, who helped this novel sing a little more every step of the way.

I want to thank my agent, Marly Rusoff, who sets the standard for representation and to whom I am so grateful for her wisdom, counsel, and advocacy.

I want to thank the Vermont College of Fine Arts Community for all your support as colleagues and friends, and allowing me to be an artist as well as your president.

I want to thank my family, my parents, my brothers and sisters, and Tia and my daughter, Sarah, for all your support of my work.

While this is not an autobiographical novel by any measure and is entirely a work of fiction, one of the pleasures of writing it was revisiting my own path toward becoming a writer, those first tentative and awkward steps I took, like Henry, many years ago. And so I want to thank, as well, those early teachers of mine: Jon Maney, Mary Caponegro, and the late Deborah Tall, who once pulled me aside and told me I had the talent to do this mysterious thing, and that made all the difference to a twenty-one-year-old writer. I also want to thank Deborah's husband, the poet David Weiss, who, with enormous kindness and generosity, once bailed me out of a thicket of trouble. I haven't forgotten.